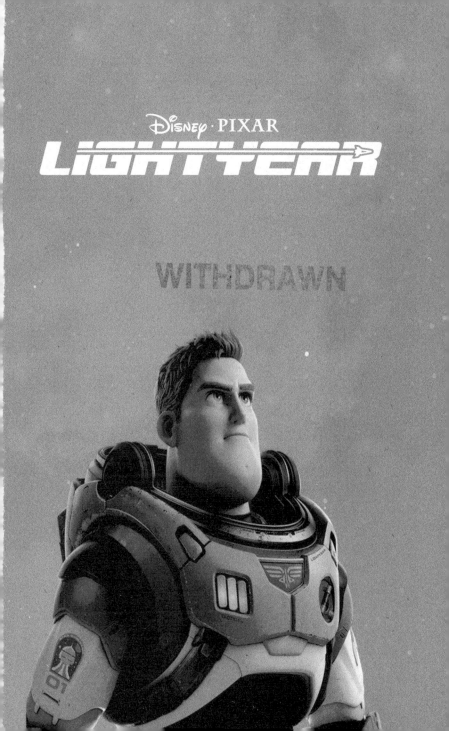

rhcbooks.com

ISBN 978-0-7364-4314-2 (hardcover)
ISBN 978-0-7364-4313-5 (paperback)

Printed in the United States of America

10 9 8 7 6 5 4 3 2 1

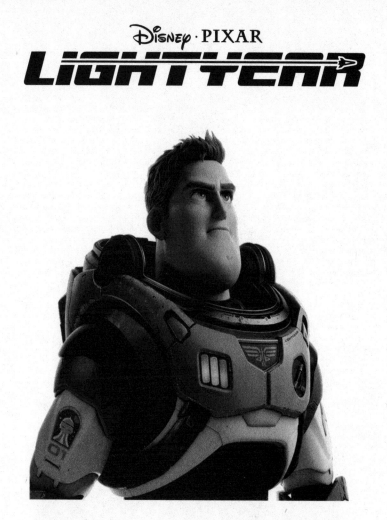

DISNEY·PIXAR
LIGHTYEAR

The Deluxe Junior Novelization

Adapted by **Meredith Rusu**

Random House 🏠 New York

Chapter 1

A hazy green mist hung low over the alien swampland, thick and still, obscuring the vegetation beneath. There was no telling what strange plants—or life—might be lurking there. Waiting. Watching. And perhaps they were, at that very moment, slithering closer to the Space Ranger's boot, which had just made its first footprint in the extraterrestrial goop.

The owner of the boot spoke into his wrist communicator. "Buzz Lightyear mission log: Star Date three-nine-oh-one." It was Captain Buzz Lightyear, Intergalactic Space Ranger. He stood tall, surveying the expanse before him, his keen gaze observing every nuance that younger, less experienced Space Rangers might overlook.

"Sensors have detected valuable resources on an uncharted planet," Buzz continued, "so we're making a detour to investigate. Space Rangers will make initial evaluations, then assess whether it's worth waking the science crew from their hypersleep . . . or simply continuing our long journey home."

Buzz allowed just the ghost of a smile to pass across his lips. He had journeyed to dozens of star systems and ventured across countless extraterrestrial terrains in the past, but something about this planet—known as T'Kani Prime—sent a thrill through him that was rare for a seasoned Space Ranger. According to their ship's computers, the unexplored swamplands of this world were teeming with potential resources that could further the crew's scientific exploration by years—or it could present danger the likes of which they had never seen. To Buzz Lightyear, everything about T'Kani Prime was new and exciting and strange.

Perhaps the planet viewed him in the same way.

Buzz pressed the toe of his boot into the bog, and the thick mud squelched with unsettling resistance. "Terrain seems a bit unstable. No readout yet, if the air is breathable. And there seems to be no sign of intelligent life anywhere."

"Who are you talking to?"

A woman's voice interrupted his report. Buzz whirled around and came face-to-face with his fellow officer Commander Alisha Hawthorne.

"No one," Buzz said, quickly lowering his wrist communicator.

"You were narrating again," Alisha said. Her tone was disapproving, but Buzz knew better. She was just teasing him.

To anyone else, Commander Alisha Hawthorne was a strict, by-the-book Space Ranger. But to Buzz Lightyear, she was the kind of friend only time could bring. The two of them had entered the academy and trained together as cadets. They had studied side by side, running drills and memorizing Star Command codes until they became second nature. Eventually, Buzz and Alisha achieved the ultimate accomplishment: joining the Space Ranger Corps. Together, they had entered the great unknown of space.

Buzz shrugged. "Just doing the mission log." He activated his laser blade to slice through a gnarled patch of swamp vines that suddenly seemed to be blocking his way. "Narrating helps me focus. Stay sharp. If it bothers you, Commander Hawthorne, I'm happy to wait back on the Turnip."

Alisha activated her own laser blade and forged a path into the jungle alongside Buzz. "Please don't call it the Turnip."

"But the ship looks like a root vegetable," Buzz pointed out.

They both glanced back at the SC-01 transport ship, its outline blurry through the haze. There was no denying that its bulbous shape did indeed give it the appearance of a turnip.

"Yes, you made that very clear at the design review," Alisha noted.

"How long have you known that I narrate?" Buzz asked as he hoisted himself up and over a cluster of vines so thick, they almost seemed like a fallen tree trunk.

"Forever," Alisha admitted with a half smile. "Since you and I were cadets. Speaking of which, you forgot to take the rookie with you."

"Ugh. Commander Hawthorne, you know how I feel about rookies," Buzz said, hacking through more vines. "They don't help. They just overcomplicate things. I'm better off doing the job myself."

"Which is why *I* brought the rookie," Alisha replied.

Only then did Buzz notice the extra figure inching cautiously behind Alisha in the muck. The rookie. In Buzz's opinion, he was an awkward, gangly cadet playing dress-up in a Space Ranger suit.

"Uh. Hello." The rookie gave a meek wave.

"No." Buzz turned away.

"Buzz," Alisha said. "Protocol requires we bring him along. Look at the rookie."

"No," Buzz repeated.

"Buzz, look at the rookie," ordered Alisha.

"No!" Buzz insisted. "He's gonna have sad eyes. You know I can't deal with the sad eyes."

"Look, look, look," said Alisha.

Against his better judgment, Buzz glanced at the rookie. Sure enough, there he was, staring at Buzz with his super-wide, eager-to-please eyes, looking pitiful, like a small child. Or a puppy.

"All right!" Buzz groaned. "You win. Look, Feather . . . Featherings . . . Feather . . ." Buzz squinted as he tried to make heads or tails of the long and complicated last name stamped on the rookie's dog tags.

"It's Featheringhamstan, sir," the rookie said eagerly.

"Look, rookie." Buzz's voice was tight. "First, you will not speak unless spoken to."

"Yes, sir!" said the rookie.

"Still talking," Buzz reminded him. "Second, respect the suit. This suit means something. It's not just protecting your body; it's protecting the universe. This suit is a promise to the world that you, and you alone, will do one thing above all: finish the mission. No matter the cost, you will never quit. Whatever the galaxy may throw your way— Will you please turn that off!"

Buzz huffed as he turned to Alisha, who had begun playing triumphant fanfare music from her

Space Ranger suit chest panel. Alisha dialed down the volume, slowly, until the music faded and the only sound remaining was the sway and slither of the alien vines.

"It's just too easy," Alisha laughed.

"You're mocking me, aren't you?" said Buzz, unamused.

"Yes, but in a supportive way," Alisha replied.

"Look, what I'm trying to say, commander," Buzz continued, "is that you and I have this job down—"

"Uh, sir?" the rookie said behind him.

"Still talking," Buzz rebuked him, still looking at Alisha. "At any moment, I know what you're thinking. I know where you're going to be. But this guy, I don't know—"

Buzz finally turned.

The rookie was gone.

And in his place was a slithering pool of vine tentacles, reaching ominously toward the two Space Rangers who didn't belong on this planet.

Chapter 2

"Vines!" Alisha cried. The swampland around them had sprung to life, with hundreds of squelchy extraterrestrial vines all attacking at once.

A low hum began vibrating in the hazy green mist.

"Bugs!" Alisha shouted as a swarm of giant insects descended upon them.

Buzz whipped around and realized with a flash of alarm that their ship was being sucked into the ground.

"The ship!" he warned. "It's sinking!"

"Everyone back to the Turnip!" Alisha commanded.

"Oh, so we're calling it the Turnip now?" Buzz said as they sprinted toward the ship.

But they were quickly overtaken by bugs.

"Engage stealth mode!" Alisha exclaimed. "It should buy us just enough time."

Alisha and Buzz pressed a button on their suits

and disappeared under stealth mode. But the protection soon ran out of power. As the duo reappeared for all the bugs to see, they realized they had only one option. In perfect unison, they ignited their laser blades and sliced their way through the attacking predators. Each had the other's back. As a bug would swoop, Buzz would blast it away with his wrist laser, turning just in time for Alisha to sever a vine that was grasping for his outstretched arm. They were performing a precise Space Ranger ballet of jumps and ducks and blasts, each knowing the other's move before they had even performed it. Vine by vine, bug by bug, they battled their way back to the Turnip and slammed shoulder to shoulder into their ship's landing elevator. It began filling with swamp mud and then short-circuited.

"Blast!" Buzz cried as he tried to operate the mud-splattered control panel.

"Here, I can reroute it," Alisha said. She ripped open the panel and began expertly rewiring the controls.

In times like these, Buzz was grateful to have such a cool-and-collected partner at his side. A rookie could never have—

Buzz paused. "Where is the—"

"Help!" the rookie suddenly screamed. The poor kid was being simultaneously carried off into the sky by a bug *and* dragged down to the ground by a vine in a terrible tug-of-war in which the rookie was the rope.

Buzz sprinted forward and sliced through the vine trapping the rookie's leg. Without missing a beat, he grabbed the kid's outstretched hand to keep him from being carried off by the bug. But the bug wasn't giving up that easily. It flicked its iridescent wing at Buzz, knocking the laser blade from the Space Ranger's hand. Then a vine snaked a tentacle around Buzz's waist and hoisted him into the air.

"No!" Alisha shouted. She fired her laser blaster at the bug—a direct hit! The creature shrieked and dropped Buzz and the rookie down into the oozing bog. But they weren't safe yet. Three more vines stretched up from the ground, encircling Buzz and the rookie to drag them to a squelchy demise.

"Buzz!" cried Alisha.

Buzz looked at his commander, and they both knew what to do. But they had only one shot.

Buzz reached out his hand just as Alisha drew back hers, prepared to throw her laser blade.

"Now!" cried Buzz.

With perfect aim, Alisha hurled the blade to Buzz. He caught it just as the vines dragged him and the rookie beneath the surface.

Alisha sucked in her breath. A moment passed that felt way too long. And then . . .

Buzz burst out of the pile of vines, holding the glowing laser blade high in triumph. Heroically, he swung the exhausted rookie over his shoulder and charged back to the ship, slamming inside the closing elevator doors just in time.

"I'll go to the engine room," Alisha announced as the muddy elevator took them to the bridge.

"I'll take the helm," Buzz said.

"And I will—" the rookie started.

"Do nothing!" Buzz commanded him sharply. "I've got this!"

Buzz leaped into one of the two captain's chairs, and the autopilot instantly chimed to life.

"How may I assist you?" it asked cheerily.

"Ugh, autopilots," Buzz groaned. If there was one thing Buzz trusted even less than rookies, it was autopilots. He confidently took hold of the control wheel on the console.

Normally, two pilots worked together to command the ship. But at the moment, it was crucial for Alisha to monitor the engine room. It was possible for Buzz to rely on the autopilot to pick up the slack . . . but if anyone could fly the Turnip off this hostile planet solo, it was him. Buzz Lightyear.

"Is there anything I can do, sir?" the rookie asked, timidly reaching toward the copilot controls.

"No!" Buzz smacked his hand away. "This is

not a simulation!" Then Buzz spoke into his radio. "Commander, status?"

Alisha's staticky voice came over the radio. "Fuel engaged. All systems go!"

Buzz punched the launch button, and the Turnip's engines blasted to life. But an unsettling groan shuddered through the ship. The resistance from the mud was strong. The Turnip lifted off awkwardly, battling to rise as if escaping quicksand.

"Warning. Launch trajectory unsound," the computer announced.

Something was wrong. The Turnip's forward trajectory had kicked in, but they weren't gaining altitude.

Buzz felt an angry bead of sweat drip down the side of his temple as he pulled hard on the wheel. The Turnip was flying almost parallel to the ground, and there wasn't a lot of time. Straight ahead, a massive mountain rose from the swampland. Buzz needed to get this ship higher—now!

"Collision imminent," said the computer. "Abort. Abort. Abort."

Buzz turned off the autopilot.

"Captain Lightyear, do you need my help?" the rookie asked, clinging to the back of Alisha's empty copilot chair as the ship lurched to one side.

"Negative!"

"Are you sure?"

"I'm Buzz Lightyear," Buzz said through gritted teeth. "I'm always sure."

Finally, the ship began to climb! The mountain was getting closer, but the ship was rising higher. They were almost up and over the mountain. They were going to make it!

CRASH!

At the last second, the underbelly of the ship snagged the peak of the mountain. Buzz heard the horrible screeching sound of metal being ripped apart—and then a big boom. A pit formed in his stomach. He knew what that second sound meant.

Chaos erupted.

The bridge was engulfed in a cacophony of warning sirens and flashing lights. They were losing altitude fast. Buzz strived to regain control, but everything was wrong. The Turnip hurtled back toward the swampland, the ground racing up to meet them as the ship crashed belly-first in a massive rupture of mud and muck.

"It's bad, Buzz." Alisha emerged from the wreckage of the engine room, covered in soot, holding a shattered fuel cell. Buzz stared at it, numb, while the rest of the crew engaged in emergency evacuation protocol around him. Thankfully, the crew's hypersleep pods had protected them during the crash. Everyone had survived. But the ship had not.

"Our hyperspeed crystal was totally destroyed," Alisha said. "Long story short . . . we're marooned."

Buzz let those words sink in. It was like a bad dream. Just an hour ago, they had been finishing up their last assignment of a five-year mission before heading home. Now everything had changed. Would they ever get home? *Could* they ever get home? This was all terribly wrong.

And it was Buzz's fault.

Dejectedly, Buzz removed the nameplate from his suit and handed it to Alisha.

"What are you doing?" Alisha asked, confused.

"I'm court-martialing myself," Buzz said. "Commander Hawthorne, I hereby relieve myself of all Space Ranger duties. This was my fault, and these people deserve better. You can throw me in the brig."

"Finish the mission, Buzz." Alisha put her hand on his shoulder. "*That's* what we do. We're not done until everyone gets home."

"But we have no fuel crystal," Buzz protested.

"So we mine the resources of this planet—create a new crystal," Alisha told him.

Buzz frowned and shook his head. "Crystallic fusion is highly unstable."

"Then we test it," Alisha countered.

Buzz felt like his head was swimming. "It's too dangerous. Manufacturing a crystal capable of hyper-speed is like . . . like trying to lasso the sun. Then someone has to attach that sun to a ship. And then that ship needs someone to fly it without blowing themselves into oblivion. Who in their right mind would— Ohhh . . ."

Alisha smirked at Buzz as he finally caught on. She slapped the nameplate back on his suit while he furrowed his brow in determination.

Chapter 3

"Buzz Lightyear mission log: Star Date three-nine-oh-two. After a full year of being marooned, our specialized crew and robotic assistants have put this planet's vast resources to incredible use. Finally, our first hyperspeed test flight is a go."

Buzz threw open the door from the locker room, letting the sunshine blast upon him.

The crowd cheered as Buzz hopped aboard a truck that was waiting to take him to the launchpad. He gazed at the fruits of his crew's yearlong efforts: perimeter fences surrounded their encampment to keep vines out. A patrol had been established to protect them from daily attacks. It hadn't been easy, but they had managed to make T'Kani Prime livable. Hospitable, even. Except for the days when the vines were feeling extra grabby. Buzz had to admit, the resources on T'Kani Prime were immeasurable. They had even managed to mine ore from the dark side of the planet to build a rudimentary space station. Crew members had individual living quarters. Some had started referring to this planet as "home."

But not Buzz. That day, he would finally finish the mission.

His truck pulled up to the launchpad, where the biggest achievement of the year awaited: the XL-1, a ship that was capable of reaching hyperspeed. The initial test flight was scheduled for today, and, according to their calculations, it should take only about four minutes. But those would be the four most important minutes of Buzz's life.

"Ready, Captain Lightyear?"

Alisha stood at the edge of the launchpad, her gaze fixed on Buzz, rather than the spaceship. Buzz could see she was worried. The stakes were high—and so was the risk. But if anyone could lasso the sun, it was Buzz Lightyear.

"Ready as I'll ever be, Commander Hawthorne."

Alisha held out an index finger. "To infinity . . ."

". . . and beyond," finished Buzz.

Buzz tapped his finger to hers, and together they "boomed" their hands apart like a mini explosion. Neither of them could remember when they had started this small ritual, but it must have been during their cadet years. It was second nature now, like a handshake or a hug.

A young crew member named Díaz came running up. "Captain Lightyear! We're all ready when you are, sir."

"A year of work for a four-minute flight," Buzz marveled. "Isn't that something?"

"Ha! Sure is!" Díaz agreed.

Buzz squared his shoulders. "Well, let's go find out if this new hyperspeed fuel is stable, so I can get us off this rock."

"Oh! Almost forgot!" Díaz handed Buzz a small computer. "Here's your IVAN, sir. Fully loaded."

Buzz rolled his eyes. IVAN—an Internal Voice-Activated Navigator—was an autopilot. The last thing he needed for the most important mission of his life was an autopilot.

Next, Díaz led Buzz to a sophisticated fuel station where Everyday Robotic Industrial Colleagues— otherwise known as ERICs—were carefully combining chemicals to concoct the perfect formula. Buzz bent down low, the blue glow of the fuel reflecting off his white space suit.

"So, this is the fuel that's gonna reach hyperspeed?" he asked.

"It has an eighty-seven-point-six percent chance," an ERIC replied.

Buzz nodded. "I'll take those odds."

Buzz and Alisha watched the ERICs load the fuel

cell into the XL-1's fuel compartment. Then Alisha went to Mission Control while Buzz climbed aboard the ship and strapped in.

"XL-1 to Mission Control. Do you copy?" he said into his radio.

"Copy, XL-1," Alisha replied. "I'm going to grant you four minutes to be off-planet, but then you come right back to us. That's an order."

Buzz smiled. "Roger that." He took a deep breath and gazed out the clear dome windshield to the waiting sky above. "Hyperspeed, here I come."

Buzz braced himself as the launch sequence initiated.

A steady computer voice counted down. "T-minus ten . . . nine . . . eight . . ." The ship began vibrating with bone-shaking intensity. "Three . . . two . . . one. Launch."

Buzz was thrust back against his seat with intense force, his teeth clattering together hard enough to numb his entire face. The pressure was massive. It was both exhilarating and terrifying at the same time.

His crew's makeshift space station grew smaller beneath him as the XL-1 rocketed into the sky and reached the upper atmosphere. Then, in a breathtaking heartbeat, the vibrating ceased, and the blackness of space enveloped the ship. Buzz exhaled.

He was back where a Space Ranger belonged—among the stars. Now for the real test.

"IVAN, pull up the flight plan, please," Buzz commanded.

"Hello—*BZZZZT*—I am your—*BZZZZT*—" IVAN fritzed.

"Ugh, autopilots!" Buzz removed IVAN from the console and blew into the cartridge. Then he replaced it.

"Hello, I am your Internal Voice-Activated Navigator," the computer said, smoothly now. "Call me IVAN."

"Ready the flight plan, please, IVAN," Buzz instructed.

"Certainly. Your mission is to accelerate through deep space, slingshot around Alpha T'Kani, then through the deceleration rings and back here to T'Kani Prime. Target flight time: four minutes, twenty-eight seconds."

Buzz nodded. "Initiating hyperlaunch." He pressed a glowing green button and the ship lurched forward, a streak of shining silver slicing through the blackness of space.

"Approaching fifty-percent hyperspeed," IVAN announced.

Buzz checked the fuel-stability readout. "Fuel stable. Increasing speed to point-six-c."

Buzz pushed the throttle. It hummed as the ship gained momentum.

"Sixty-percent hyperspeed," IVAN announced.

The brilliant glow of Alpha T'Kani grew brighter and brighter as his ship flew impossibly fast toward the star. Buzz's heart pounded. The XL-1 whipped around the star, using its gravitational force to perfectly slingshot around and turn back toward home.

He was halfway there. This was going to work.

"Approaching point-eight-c," he confirmed. "Pushing to hyperspeed."

Buzz gripped the throttle and forced it forward.

BOOM!

An explosion ripped through the hull! Alarms wailed.

"Failure in engine one," said IVAN. "Fuel cell unstable."

"IVAN, status!" Buzz yelled.

"Trajectory error: plus four degrees."

Buzz looked at the projected path on the dashboard screen. The explosion had pushed them off-course. The ship was veering away from T'Kani Prime.

"Failure to course-correct will result in missing the rings. We'll fly off into deep space, resulting in certain death," IVAN explained.

"Yes, thank you," Buzz said.

"Ejection is your only option," IVAN stated, popping open the cover to a glowing red eject button.

"No, no," Buzz shot back, slamming the cover closed. "I can do it."

He grabbed a circular slide rule and a grease pencil to work out flight calculations on the canopy of the ship. He could fix this—he was sure he could. It was just like a crisis simulation from his cadet days. He could solve the course-correction calculation by hand and get them back home. He didn't need an autopilot to tell him it was impossible. Nothing was impossible—not for Buzz Lightyear.

"Warning: You have twenty-six seconds to course-correct," IVAN said. "You now have twenty-five seconds to course-correct."

"Stop counting, please," Buzz snapped. His calculations were close—he needed to focus.

"Mission failure imminent," IVAN stated. "Please record your last words."

"Not today, IVAN!" shouted Buzz.

"Not today, IVAN!" IVAN repeated. "If you are satisfied with this recording, speak or select one."

Buzz circled his answer and slammed the grease pencil down. "IVAN, push the engines all the way! Maximum power!"

"That action is inadvisable," IVAN said. "Fuel-cell detonation—"

"Is exactly what I'm counting on," Buzz interrupted.

IVAN did as it was told. The vibration from the ship was nearly uncontrollable—it was going to tear apart.

"Open the fuel door!" Buzz yelled urgently.

IVAN complied. The fuel door sprang open, and through the windshield, Buzz could see the dangerous blue glow of the volatile fuel crystal illuminating the ship. He flipped up the safety cap and hovered his hand over the button labeled EJECT FUEL CELL.

"Detonation in five . . . four . . . three . . . two . . . one . . ."

"NOW!" Buzz commanded as he smashed his finger on the button.

The fuel cell ejected, and a millisecond later . . .

KA-BOOM!

The detonation ripped through space, its explosive force knocking Buzz's ship to the right . . . exactly four degrees.

Buzz was pinned back against his seat as the ship hurtled toward T'Kani Prime. Miraculously, the deceleration rings caught the vessel and slowed its momentum. But without a fuel cell to power the ship, Buzz was helpless to control the XL-1 as it plummeted back toward the planet.

"Course corrected. You failed to reach hyperspeed," IVAN announced.

"I didn't need to hear that, IVAN."

"You didn't hear that? I'm sorry. I'll repeat."

"No, I meant—I didn't need to—"

"You failed to reach hyperspeed."

"Thank you, IVAN."

"I said—"

Buzz shut off IVAN and braced for impact as the ship barreled to the ground, the burning scent of scorched metal overwhelming his senses.

Finally, he landed. Buzz opened the visor on his helmet and slouched back in his seat. He was alive. He jumped out of the cockpit and saw a figure running up to him.

"Captain!" the figure cried. It was Díaz. "Are you okay?"

Buzz had just begun to nod when he noticed something strange. Díaz was different. His hair was long, and he had a goatee.

"Whoa, Díaz," Buzz said, confused. "You grew a beard. How did you grow a beard?"

"Oh, right." Díaz stroked the goatee on his chin. "Uh, first off, welcome back. Secondly—"

"Wait," Buzz interrupted, looking over Díaz's shoulder. The command base was different, too—larger, with an entirely new building constructed to one side.

"What is this?" Buzz asked, an unsettling feeling growing in his chest. "How long was I gone?"

Díaz paused before answering. "Four years, two months, and three days."

Chapter 4

"We thought we'd lost you, Buzz." Alisha hugged her old friend with a ferocity that startled even the seasoned Space Ranger.

"Alisha," Buzz said, shaken. "What happened?"

Alisha looked Buzz in the eye. "Time dilation."

She took Buzz to the hangar where an ERIC had mapped out mathematical equations on a chalkboard.

"Time dilation is quite simple," ERIC explained. "As you approached hyperspeed, your time slowed relative to our own. So, during your mission, you aged only minutes while the rest of us have aged years."

Buzz studied the math, deep in thought.

"Simply put," ERIC continued, "the faster you fly—"

"The faster I fly, the further into the future I travel," Buzz interjected. "I get it."

Buzz walked out of the hangar with Alisha close behind. "So, what are we going to do now?"

"I don't know," Alisha admitted. "But I think we should hold off on any more test flights until we figure out something else."

"Commander," Buzz protested. "We said 'finish the mission.' That's what Space Rangers do."

"At what cost, Buzz?" Alisha asked. "Are you willing to lose another four years?"

For once, Buzz didn't have an answer. He took in her expression—the creases that etched her brow and the way the corners of her mouth sagged ever so slightly in a weary frown that he wasn't used to seeing on her face. These weren't the consequences of age, Buzz realized with a pang. They were from grief. He may have felt like he'd been gone for only four minutes, but Alisha had been carrying the weight of losing her best friend for four *years*.

Alisha offered to drive Buzz home. He was unusually quiet during the ride to the crew compound. Accepting failure wasn't in the code of being a Space Ranger. This new hurdle—this new problem—felt like one he alone needed to solve. He just needed time. And that was the one thing working against him.

"So everyone is just stuck here. Because of me," he said bitterly as they reached their quarters.

"Hey . . . you all right?" Alisha asked him, clearly worried about her friend.

"Yeah," Buzz said, trying to brush away his dark

mood. Sulking wasn't in the code of a Space Ranger, either.

That was when he noticed the light glint off a sparkly ring on Alisha's hand.

"Wait—what's that?" he asked, pointing to it.

"Oh, I got engaged!" Alisha revealed.

"Wow! That's—that's great!" Buzz said, feeling a mixture of happiness and surprise. "What's her name?"

"Kiko," Alisha told him proudly. "She's one of the science crew. It's funny. I never would have met her if we hadn't been stranded."

"You got engaged to someone you just met?" Buzz asked, confused.

"Buzz, I met her three years ago," Alisha said gently.

"Oh, right . . . right." He pointed at Alisha's door. "Well, congratulations. I'd love to meet her."

Alisha smiled. "There's plenty of time for that. Get some rest. That's an order."

She swiped her ID card to enter her apartment. And then Buzz was alone.

He sighed and swiped his own card, plodding heavily into his quarters. He glanced down and noticed an unopened Star Command box on the floor. On top was a note: *You're welcome! Alisha.*

He knelt to open it, removing the cardboard

packaging to reveal a small mechanical mouse and an adorable robotic cat.

"Uhhh . . . ," Buzz said, confused.

"Hello, Buzz." The cat suddenly opened its eyes.

"Ack!" Buzz jumped, startled. The cat hopped out of his arms and sat in front of him.

"I am Sox, your personal companion robot," the cat informed him.

"My what?" Buzz asked.

"I was issued by Star Command to ease your emotional transition after your time away," Sox explained, swishing his tail rhythmically.

"Oh . . . uh . . . well," Buzz stammered. "That's very considerate of you, robot feline. But . . . no. No, thank you."

"I'm afraid it's protocol," Sox said. "Sensors indicate you've missed four birthdays. Would you like a frosted snack cake to celebrate?"

Buzz shook his head as he opened his kitchen's cabinets and selected a freeze-dried meal. "Negative. That would compromise my nutritional regimen." He shook the box until the food heated and expanded.

"We can talk about your feelings," Sox suggested. "I am an excellent listener."

"No, no." Buzz shook his head between bites.

"Look, I've had a really long—" Buzz paused. "Day? And it did not go as planned."

Sox's round eyes grew rounder. "The mission was unsuccessful?"

Buzz nodded. "Affirmative."

"Oh, no," Sox said with genuine sympathy. "I am so sorry to hear that."

Buzz looked at the little cat. Somehow, its shiny robotic eyes seemed to glisten with real emotion. It was strangely comforting.

"Thank you, Sox."

"You're welcome, Buzz. Shall we play a game?"

"No, thank you."

Sox wasn't ready to give up. "I can create a game specifically for you based on your exact personality profile."

Buzz walked toward the bed. "Hey listen, Sox, buddy. I'm pretty tired. So I'm gonna go ahead and hit the rack."

"Of course," said Sox. "I can provide sleep sounds if you like. I have several options. Summer night. Ocean paradise. Whale calls!"

"No, no," Buzz said, collapsing onto the bed. "White noise is fine."

"Very well," Sox replied. He hopped up onto Buzz's nightstand.

Buzz wearily closed his eyes. "Good night, Sox."

"Good night, Buzz," Sox replied. Then he began to emit a steady hum of white noise that blocked all extraneous sound.

The Turnip was flying almost parallel to the ground, and there wasn't a lot of time. Straight ahead was a massive mountain.

"Uh, Captain Lightyear, do you need any help?" the rookie asked from behind Buzz.

"No! I can do it!" Buzz gripped the control wheel and pulled with all his might. He needed to get this ship higher now or they were going to crash.

Desperately, he reached over to the second wheel. If he could just pull both together, they'd gain altitude. But the more he strained, the farther away the second wheel seemed to be.

He heard a woman's voice. "Buzz?"

Buzz turned around. Instead of the rookie, it was Alisha who stood behind him.

"Are you sure?" she asked.

"I can do it!" Buzz shot up in bed, his heart racing. He was drenched in cold sweat.

Confused, he looked around the darkened room. There was his dresser. His window. The sleek white décor of Star Command living quarters. And gradually, his breathing slowed.

Sox stopped his white noise from the nightstand and tilted his head. "Sensors indicate you had a nightmare. Would you like to talk about it?"

"Negative," Buzz sighed.

"Okay," replied Sox. "But remember, my mission is to help you. And I'm not giving up on my mission."

Buzz looked at the little robotic cat. "Yeah," he mumbled. He wiped the clammy moisture from his forehead and clenched his fist. He didn't like feeling like this. Uncertain. Frightened. Helpless. This wasn't *him*. Buzz Lightyear, Space Ranger, found hope where there was none. Illuminated pathways out of danger when all else seemed lost. Buzz Lightyear, Space Ranger, was the captain everyone else looked to when they needed a leader to make the tough choices that would get them home.

Buzz Lightyear, Space Ranger, *always* finished the mission.

"Yeah. You know what, Sox?" Buzz gazed out the window where Alpha T'Kani was just rising over the horizon. "I'm not giving up on my mission, either!"

"Great!" Sox followed Buzz to the kitchen. "So what can I do?"

"Why don't you engage with your mouse buddy?"

Buzz said between bites of a freeze-dried breakfast supplement.

Sox looked doubtfully at the little mouse puttering around on the kitchen floor. "Is there anything more . . . challenging?"

"You want a challenge?" Buzz asked, still chewing his breakfast. "Okay . . . I guess you could work on this fuel-stability thing."

He presented Sox with a small computer tablet that held all the latest research on the hyperspeed fuel crystal.

"Crystallic fusion. Of course," Sox said in wonder. He began typing on the computer's keyboard.

Meanwhile, Buzz grabbed his gear and headed for the door.

"When should I expect you back?" Sox asked.

Buzz glanced over his shoulder and smiled. "About four years."

"Hold on! You don't have to do this!" The urgency in Alisha's voice was drowned out by the mechanical whirring of an ERIC preparing another fuel mixture. Buzz stood at attention, already geared up in his test flight suit.

"Commander, this is my mistake," Buzz said. "I need to make it right."

Buzz's determination elicited a spark of hope inside Alisha that she hadn't felt in . . . a long time. She'd almost forgotten what it had been like to be a Space Ranger. Four years of adapting to life on a hostile alien planet had dulled her sense of adventure. And risk. But Buzz had awakened something in her, like a memory from a life left behind. Maybe Buzz could help them get that life back.

"Okay," she said, resigned. "But maybe we should think about this." She watched as Buzz loaded the fuel cell into the XL-2 and climbed into the cockpit.

"Think about what?" Buzz asked. "Come on, we're Space Rangers."

"Would be nice to wear the suit again," Alisha mused. "People are starting to forget Space Rangers ever mattered."

Buzz shut the visor on his helmet with a solid click. "Well, I'm about to fix that." He held out his finger. "To infinity . . ."

Alisha studied her friend's face for a long beat. She wouldn't see this face for four years.

She touched her finger to his. ". . . and beyond."

Chapter 5

Buzz had no way of knowing what the future held. Even a Space Ranger couldn't predict that. But his determination was strong. He never let go of the undying faith that if he tried hard enough, he could eventually succeed.

Maybe that was why after the XL-2 mission failed the same way the first one had, he pushed for an XL-3. And then an XL-4. And then another. Four heart-pounding minutes each time for him. Four years of life for the crew back on T'Kani Prime.

Alisha had been right: the memory of Space Rangers and what they represented had all but faded throughout the base. The crew went about their business, hardly giving thought to the lone Space Ranger out there—somewhere—on a mission to get them back home.

But Alisha never forgot. She was always there to greet Buzz in her office, offering him a warm hug and a hero's welcome. After the XL-2, Buzz returned to discover that Alisha was expecting a baby with Kiko. Four years after that, Buzz met her son, Avery. Four years, and four years, and another four more. Avery graduated from high school. Alisha and Kiko celebrated a milestone anniversary.

Everything changed around Buzz, but there was always Alisha, at her desk, waiting to greet him. Each time Buzz entered her office, he stood a little taller when he saw the Space Ranger suit still proudly displayed next to her chair. It, at least, looked the same, even as its owner grew older beside it.

One day after another failed mission, Buzz trudged down the hallway toward Alisha's office. Another failure. Another fuel crystal that got so close to working before shattering in a terrific explosion.

But when Buzz opened Alisha's office door, the room was empty. No photos. No Space Ranger suit. No Alisha.

Just a desk with a small electronic device labeled BUZZ resting on top.

With a cold fear creeping over him, Buzz inserted a chip attached to the note into the device. A hologram of Alisha appeared. Buzz gasped. The image of his friend was one he hardly recognized. In it, she was old and weak, propped up on pillows in a hospital bed.

Alisha smiled feebly at him in the recording.

"Hi, Buzz," she said. "You'll be back here in a year or two. And, well . . . I won't." Alisha smiled sadly. "I don't know when it happened, but I seem to have gone and gotten very old."

Tears misted Buzz's vision as he continued to watch.

"I always thought we'd get to be Space Rangers again," Alisha admitted. "I missed being out among the stars. All the adventures. But more than any of that . . . I missed you."

Then a young girl bounded into the frame of the hologram projection. She was wearing a homemade Space Ranger suit.

"Hi, Grandma!" she exclaimed.

Alisha hugged the child. "Hey, sweetheart. I'm leaving a message for my friend Buzz."

The little girl gasped. "The Space Ranger?"

"That's right. He's in space right now."

"Wow!" Izzy exclaimed in wonder.

Alisha looked back at the camera. "This is my granddaughter, Izzy."

"I'm gonna be a Space Ranger, too!" Izzy announced to Buzz, puffing out her chest.

"Just like him?" Alisha asked.

Izzy shook her head. "Just like you."

Alisha squeezed her granddaughter tight. Then she sighed and smiled. She turned to look at Buzz one final time.

"Goodbye, Buzz," she said. "I'm sorry I won't be there to see you finish the mission."

She extended her pointer finger toward the camera. "To infinity . . ."

Buzz touched the hologram. His finger passed through it slightly so that their hands melded into one. ". . . and beyond."

The recording ended, and the hologram disappeared. Buzz was alone. He looked down and noticed a white piece of paper stuck under the desk. He flipped it over to see a photo of himself and Alisha in their Space Ranger suits. Two young cadets, grinning with unbridled optimism, their heads filled with dreams of adventure and glory among the stars.

A single tear fell onto the photo.

Suddenly, a knock and a carefree voice rang out behind Buzz, echoing off the empty office walls. Shaken, Buzz turned.

A tall man dressed in a commander uniform pushed a rolling chair piled high with moving boxes into the office.

"Sorry to interrupt!" the man said. "I'm just

moving into my new—" He gasped. "Look at that! The actual Buzz Lightyear in the flesh!" He saluted.

Buzz returned the gesture absentmindedly. "Affirmative," he mumbled.

"Commander Cal Burnside. I was a big fan of yours when I was a kid."

Buzz tried to shake himself out of his daze. He wanted to grieve. But a Space Ranger didn't do that in the presence of a commander. There would be time to process his emotions later, in private. He needed to focus on the mission.

"Then I look forward to working with you to finally get us out of here," he said, squaring his shoulders.

"Oh . . . uh, did no one tell you?" Commander Burnside fidgeted nervously. "We're shutting down the program."

The words sucked Buzz's breath away. "What?"

"We've decided we're gonna go ahead and stay right here," Commander Burnside informed him.

"Wait, *here?*" Buzz said incredulously.

Commander Burnside brightened, like he had the solution to a big problem. He showed Buzz a hologram of the base surrounded by a laser shield.

"It'll keep all the critters out!" Commander Burnside said enthusiastically. "And we'll just tuck right in here and make do with what we've got."

Burnside started to lead Buzz to the door. "No,

wait, you don't understand, commander," said Buzz. "I can still do it! I can get us out of here."

"Man, it's great you still believe that!" Burnside said, as if complimenting a young child's artwork. "But we're good, Buzz. Got the laser shield!"

Then he closed the door on a stunned Buzz.

Later, Buzz gazed out the window of his quarters. In his hand was the old photo of him and Alisha.

In the distance, he watched workers haul long metal bars to construct the framework for the new laser shield. A steel grid to lock the bugs out . . . and lock the crew in. A prison they were building with gusto, one bar at a time.

Buzz hung his head. How had this all gone so horribly wrong?

"Buzz?"

Sox softly came up beside his Space Ranger companion. "I've got some good news, Buzz. I figured out the fuel problem."

"What?" said Buzz, breaking out of his reverie.

"It was an interesting combination," Sox explained. "Just the slightest variance. But it made all the difference."

Buzz watched as Sox brought up a hologram of the crystallic fusion formula, highlighting a green element that when activated, caused the crystal to glow with a rainbow of colors.

"Sox . . . ," Buzz breathed in disbelief. "How did you do this?"

"It took me sixty-two years, seven months, and five days," Sox replied.

"And it's stable?" Buzz asked, a fractal of hope crystalizing inside him.

Sox nodded. "Theoretically. I look forward to finding out. On your next mission."

Buzz couldn't believe it. All those years, the result had always been the same. Nothing had ever moved the needle. And now, finally—this was it. The missing piece of the puzzle.

A heavy knock on Buzz's door startled both the Space Ranger and Sox from their discussion.

Buzz opened it to find two Star Command security guards.

"Evening, captain. We're here to pick up your companion robot."

Buzz blinked. "What do you mean?"

"Security purposes," one of the guards stated. "You understand."

Buzz frowned. "No, actually, I don't."

The other guard held up a cat carrier. "We're shutting down the program, so . . . we have to decommission your cat."

The guards moved toward the door, but Buzz blocked their way.

"Now, hold on!" Buzz exclaimed. "Just—"

The guards grunted, and Buzz looked them up and down. They were physically intimidating and equipped with security gear. Buzz may have been a skilled combatant, but he wasn't going to win a fight in his sweatpants. Still, he couldn't let them decommission Sox like an old piece of hardware. And not when they were so close to finally having a solution!

"At least let me do it," Buzz sighed.

He took the cat carrier and closed the door. The guards waited outside. Suddenly, the guards heard a loud crash. They burst through the door and were greeted by the sight of the empty cat carrier on the floor, a window shattered, and Buzz and Sox gone.

Chapter 6

"Uh, Buzz, where are we going?" Sox asked, his usually even voice indicating robotic concern as they sped off in Buzz's truck toward the Star Command base.

"We're going to space!" Buzz announced.

"*What?*" exclaimed Sox.

Buzz skidded up to the launchpad, grabbed Sox, and raced into the locker room. He suited up and activated his wrist recorder. "Buzz Lightyear mission log: Star Date . . . I have no idea. In possession of stable fuel formula. I plan to reach hyperspeed, and this time finally finish the mission."

"Who ya talking to, Buzz?" Sox asked.

"Doesn't matter," Buzz said.

Together, they snuck toward the launchpad elevator.

"Buzz," Sox said seriously, "my programming

compels me to notify Star Command that you have gone—"

"Star Command was going to decommission you," Buzz interrupted.

Sox froze. "What?"

"That's right." Buzz nodded. "Lights out. No more Sox."

Just then, the elevator door opened—right in front of a security guard!

"Hey!" the shocked guard exclaimed. "You're not authorized to be in this area—"

Sox opened his mouth and shot a tranquilizer dart at the guard. She collapsed on the floor, immediately asleep.

"Whoa," Buzz said, impressed. "I didn't know you could do that." He paused. "Wait a minute. Was that for me? In case I got out of line?"

Sox looked at Buzz. "I bought you five minutes."

Together, they hastily made their way to the fuel depot. Normally, ERICs would be rolling about, mixing the formulas. But the depot was empty. Not one mechanical helper was in sight.

Sox pulled up the stable fuel formula. Carefully, Buzz filled the fuel cell according to Sox's exact instructions.

"Okay, here goes," Buzz said, lifting the handle of

the fuel cell. The liquid inside turned into a multi-colored crystal that refracted rainbows of light. Buzz could already see that this fuel crystal was different from the others.

Suddenly, a door slammed nearby, and a guard began sweeping the area with a flashlight. Buzz leaned back, knocking over the tablet with the formula.

"The formula!" Sox gasped.

The tablet lay broken on the ground. But Buzz couldn't worry about that. He grabbed the fuel cell and Sox and ran to the nearest ship.

The XL-15 was covered with a tarp. Buzz inserted the precious fuel crystal into the fuel port, then he and Sox climbed into the cockpit.

"Tango to base! Tango to base! Security breach in the launch bay!" another guard shouted into his radio.

"Blast!" Buzz whispered.

"We have a guard down! Repeat, we have a guard down!" the alarmed guard continued.

Buzz was running out of time. He quickly scanned the controls while Sox found a cozy perch behind Buzz's headrest. If they were quiet, they could power up the ship before anyone realized they were on it. Then it would be too late for Star Command to stop the liftoff.

Buzz plugged in IVAN.

"Hello!" IVAN announced loudly. "I am your Internal Voice-Activated Navigator."

"No! IVAN, no! Shhh!" Buzz said as he tried to muffle IVAN with his hands.

"Call me IVAN," the computer continued.

Suddenly, heavy footsteps thudded their way. IVAN's commotion had attracted attention!

A technician's voice came over the ship's radio. "XL-15, this is Control. Is there someone in there?"

Buzz froze and stared at the radio.

"Say something," Sox encouraged.

"XL-15? Please respond," said the technician.

"Uh, copy, Control," Buzz said, thinking fast. "Just the, uh, cleaning crew. Cleaning crew! We're cleaning the cockpit. Cleaning . . . items . . . in here?"

"Commander, did we authorize a cockpit cleaning for the XL-15?" Buzz heard the confused technician talking to her superior on the radio.

"What?" Commander Burnside's voice said in the background. "No!"

Buzz initiated the launch sequence, sending the XL-15 rolling toward the launch site. The guards arrived and began banging on the cockpit window.

"Stop right now and put your hands over your head!" one of the guards ordered.

Buzz pressed another button that elevated the ship to the vertical launch position. The guards tried to hold on, but they slid off the ship and landed on the ground in a heap.

When he thought he was in the home stretch, Buzz pressed the button for the silo doors.

"Unauthorized," IVAN said.

Buzz pressed the button again.

"Unauthorized," IVAN repeated.

Buzz noticed elite security guards from the Zap Patrol entering the hangar. He was most certainly outnumbered. "C'mon! We're sitting ducks here!" he shouted helplessly at IVAN.

"Allow me," Sox said. He climbed onto the console and the tip of his tail opened to reveal a flash drive. He plugged his tail into the port.

"Beep boop beep boop beep boop," Sox said as he over-rode the override.

Finally, the silo doors closed, and Buzz pressed the launch button. The XL-15 rocketed into the atmosphere, leaving the flashing lights and wailing alarms far beneath them.

"Lightyear!" Burnside's voice was furious over the radio. "I know you can hear me! Return the ship to base right now, or so help me—"

Buzz turned off the radio with a resounding *click*.

"Sox," he said, "let's break this hyperspeed barrier and get everyone home."

Chapter 7

"Approaching seventy-percent hyperspeed," IVAN announced as Buzz and Sox rocketed around Alpha T'Kani.

Buzz braced himself, watching the gauge steadily climb.

"Approaching eighty-percent hyperspeed," IVAN said.

Every inch of the ship rattled as the velocity increased. Normally, at this point, a huge explosion would rip through the engines, shattering Buzz's hopes of success. But things were different this time. The gauge kept climbing.

"Fuel is stable," Buzz breathed. He had never made it this far before.

"Ninety-percent hyperspeed," IVAN announced.

Buzz watched as the needle pushed further, as though it was the simplest thing in the world, until—

ZHOOOOOM!

Everything around Buzz and Sox suddenly went quiet. The ship powered forward, and Buzz's head was pinned against his seat.

"One-hundred-percent hyperspeed," IVAN announced.

Buzz strained against the force. From the corner of his eye, he could see colorful lights streaking past the ship's window, an array of glowing white, pink, and gold. The familiar lights of hyperspeed travel that Buzz hadn't seen in . . . what felt like a lifetime. Tears escaped his eyes and rolled straight back onto the headrest. Those serene, shimmering lights were the most beautiful sight Buzz had ever witnessed.

Then without warning, Buzz and Sox were thrust forward violently. The XL-15 had just passed through the first deceleration ring orbiting above T'Kani Prime. The velocity decreased with stomach-churning intensity.

FWOOM. Another impact. They had passed through the second deceleration ring, then the third. Buzz looked out the window as a hazy gray sky rolled by. Unexpectedly, a celebratory burst of confetti shot out from the control panel.

"Congratulations, Captain Lightyear," IVAN said. "You have achieved hyperspeed."

"We did it," Buzz whispered, his voice breaking in relief. "Sox, we did it!"

Sox, now gripping onto Buzz's leg after having been pushed there by the force of their acceleration, looked up with his large, round eyes. "Congratulations, Buzz," he said. "That was utterly terrifying, and I regret having joined you."

Buzz couldn't believe it. He had *finally* finished the mission. He could fix what he had broken. He could get his crew home!

Buzz checked to see how close they were to landing at the Star Command base. There it was, approaching with . . . way too much speed.

"No, no, no!" Buzz said, snapping back to Space Ranger mode.

"What is it, Buzz?" Sox asked.

Buzz pulled hard on the control wheel. "Our velocity is still extremely high."

Despite his best efforts, the ship whizzed right past the runway in a blur.

"Are we going to crash?" Sox asked.

"No!" Buzz said. "Well, technically, yes. Just hang on!"

The tiny crew braced for impact as the XL-15 careened toward the wilderness beyond the base. Buzz gripped the wheel, just barely keeping the ship under control. In a plume of dirt, the wheels of the XL-15 touched down and skidded hard to the left. For a nerve-wracking few seconds, Buzz was certain they were going to crash into the untamed swamp far beyond the perimeter. But miraculously, the XL-15 slowed to a halt just before the tree line. Buzz sank back in his seat. They had made it.

The cockpit canopy opened, and in the distance, Buzz could swear he heard a bird singing. It was more likely an alien bug chirping. But that day, it sounded sweet all the same.

"After all these years!" he exclaimed. Somewhere, he hoped that Alisha was watching. He hoped she knew that he'd kept his promise. But he hadn't done it alone. Buzz looked down at Sox with immense gratitude. "Thank you, Sox!"

With renewed energy, Buzz jumped down from the cockpit and fired his flare gun into the air. The Mission Control rescue team would be there any minute. Hopefully, having successfully achieved hyperspeed would absolve him of any ship-stealing wrongdoing.

Then he went to the fuel port on the ship and extracted the fuel cell. The crystal glowed with its rainbow of color, full of power. Buzz smiled.

"Mission log supplemental," he spoke into his wrist recorder. "After 'borrowing' a ship from Star

Command, I've achieved hyperspeed and I'm finally ready to leave this planet once and for all."

Buzz glanced out over the swampland, expecting to see a convoy already en route. But there were no signs of emergency vehicles. Everything was unnaturally still. Buzz frowned. The crew must have seen his flare gun. Where was everyone?

"Buzz Lightyear to Star Command," he said into his wrist communicator. "Come in, Star Command."

Buzz peered across the expanse just as thudding footsteps pounded up behind him. Someone tackled him and Sox to the ground!

"Hey!" Buzz exclaimed.

"Shhh!" his assailant warned. It was a woman in a full helmet and uniform. "The robots!"

"The what?" Buzz sputtered, his face splattered with mud.

"The *robots*!" the woman hissed through clenched teeth.

She pulled them behind a boulder just as a giant yellow robot emerged from the trees. Buzz had never seen anything like it. The mechanical monster was three times the size of a human, with heavy metal armor and a single red laser eye in the center of its domed head. It approached the XL-15, scanning it.

"Wait," Buzz whispered urgently. "What's it doing?"

"Shhh!" the woman said.

Buzz, Sox, and the woman watched as the robot completed its scan. Then it attached a metallic disc to the hull of the XL-15 and pressed a red button in the center. In a flash, both the robot and ship disappeared, teleported away.

"My ship!" Buzz cried, jumping up in a panic.

"Be quiet!" the woman warned.

"Where'd it go?" Buzz demanded.

The woman pointed to the sky, and Buzz looked up. He gasped. Hovering overhead was a massive alien spacecraft.

"What *is* that?" Buzz exclaimed. "What is going on?"

"Get down!" the woman ordered.

They ducked back behind the boulder as an alien space pod launched from the ship, on course for their location.

"Shoot!" the woman spat. "Come on!"

Swiftly, she led them into the dense swamp and up a hill. Her head swiveled this way and that. She knew exactly where to go.

But Buzz didn't know where they were going, or even what was going on. And he didn't like it. "Why are there robots?" he demanded. "Where did the robots come from?"

"Where did *you* come from?" the woman countered.

"I came from here!" Buzz exclaimed.

"Here?" she scoffed. Then suddenly, she stopped, as though a thought or a memory had struck her cold. She turned to him, took a step closer, and wiped the mud from his face.

"Buzz?" she whispered.

Buzz noticed her nameplate, which had the name: HAWTHORNE. The woman removed her helmet. Buzz couldn't believe his eyes. It was a face he hadn't seen a long time. One he hadn't thought he would ever see again.

"Alisha?" he asked, his voice catching.

"Oh, no," said the woman. "That's my grandmother. I'm Izzy."

"Izzy?" Buzz asked. "But—but you were just a little . . ."

He indicated the height of a small child with his hand, thinking back to the recording he'd watched just hours before in Alisha's office. Hours in his time, anyway.

A sickening realization caused his stomach to sink. "Sox, how long were we gone?"

Sox's ears turned as he gathered the data. "Twenty-two years, nineteen weeks, and four days."

Buzz's head was spinning as Izzy pulled him into a

rock cove high up on the hillside. Twenty-two years. An entire new generation had grown up on T'Kani Prime while he had been away.

He watched Izzy scan the perimeter using binoculars, her keen gaze scanning for any sign of robots. And for the briefest moment, he couldn't help feeling like he was watching Alisha, the way she had been back in their cadet days, always leading training exercises with precise confidence.

"You know, your grandma and I could practically finish each other's sentences," Buzz told her. "If you're anything like her, we're going to make—"

"—some robots cry," Izzy said.

"—a great team," said Buzz at the same time.

Buzz furrowed his brow. "Okay. So . . . get me up to speed on this."

"Right." Izzy nodded. "The Zurg ship showed up about a week ago."

"What's a Zurg?" Buzz asked.

"Oh, that's the only thing the robots say," Izzy explained. "So that's what we call the big ship. The Zurg ship arrived, the robots surrounded the base, and then, well—"

Izzy activated a hologram on her watch. Buzz saw an older version of Commander Burnside.

"Citizens of T'Kani Prime: robot aliens have attacked!" Burnside shouted. Behind him in the hologram, blasts engulfed the base as troops and robots exchanged laser fire. "Everyone, inside the perimeter! Look out!"

Burnside turned to shoot a robot coming up behind him.

"We are activating the laser shield immediately!" he said.

Then the message cut out.

"And that's the last we heard," Izzy said. She handed Buzz her binoculars, and he looked across the valley to the distant Star Command base. The glimmering laser shield enveloped the entire colony in a protective bubble while hundreds of robots unleashed relentless laser assaults.

"All those people . . . ," Buzz said, "they were counting on me. And now they're trapped."

"We've tried to reach them, but there's no communication in or out," said Izzy.

"Sox?" Buzz asked.

"Meow, meow, meow, meow." Sox's ears pivoted as he scanned the area for communication signals. "She's correct."

Izzy raised an eyebrow. "Did you just check me against your cat?"

"Well, he's not your standard-issue feline," Buzz admitted. "Actually, Sox was a gift from your grandmother."

"Hello, Izzy," Sox said.

Izzy smiled and petted Sox. "Hello, Sox."

Sox purred.

"Hey, what's that noise?" Buzz asked. "C'mon, don't break my cat."

"He's purring," Izzy said. "He likes it."

Buzz looked at his robot companion. "Sox, do you like that?"

"I do," Sox admitted.

Buzz tilted his head. "Huh." He'd had no idea.

"Well, I hope you're ready for action," Izzy said, standing. "Because all we needed was a pilot."

"For what?" Buzz asked.

Izzy smiled confidently. "I have a plan. And a team. Come on!"

Chapter 8

A short while later, Buzz and Izzy stood inside a large outpost. Waiting for them were two soldiers in full uniform with helmets, guarding a spaceship that Buzz recognized as an Armadillo.

"All right, team. Fall in!" Izzy commanded.

"Hup, hup!" The two soldiers marched forward at attention. One was very tall and the other rather short.

"Whoa," Buzz said, impressed.

"I found a pilot." Izzy grinned at her cohorts. "Operation Surprise Party is a go!"

"I like this." Buzz nodded approvingly. "An elite squad. Best of the best." Buzz motioned to Izzy. "You know, her grandmother was the greatest Space Ranger in the history of the corps. It'll be an honor to work with you."

Izzy activated a hologram showing the robots

surrounding the base and the alien ship hovering above it. "Let's review our objectives."

"Kill the robots!" the shorter soldier exclaimed.

"And don't die," added the taller soldier.

The shorter soldier huffed. "'Don't die' is just something you want to do *every* day."

"It's still an objective," the taller soldier insisted.

Buzz cleared his throat. "If I may . . . We have *one* objective." He held up the glowing fuel cell with the crystal. "We need to put this crystal in the Turnip and get out of here. That's been my mission ever since I—" He paused, realizing his new team probably had no idea what he was talking about. "Well, since before you were born. So, to do that, we need to get onto the base."

"To do that, we have to kill all the robots," the shorter soldier declared, pointing at the robots in the hologram.

"To do that, we have to destroy the Zurg ship." Izzy pointed to the alien ship hovering ominously in the hologram.

"And to do any of that, we have to *not* die," the taller soldier concluded.

"So, Operation Surprise Party," Izzy said to Buzz. "It's a variation on Operation Thunderspear. Didn't you get a medal for that one?"

"Two, actually," Buzz said proudly. "But—wait, how do you know about Operation Thunderspear?"

Izzy grinned. "I've read all my grandma's Space Ranger books from cover to cover. Twice." She pointed at her Hawthorne nameplate.

Buzz nodded, impressed yet again. He hadn't realized how much he'd missed having a confident partner. It was almost as if he were debriefing for a high-stakes Space Ranger mission, just like the old days, with Alisha Hawthorne by his side.

"We've figured out the Zurg ship powers the robots on the ground," Izzy said. "So we fly up there, we blow up the ship, and 'Surprise, robots!'"

She manipulated the hologram to show the Zurg ship blowing up and all the robots falling to the ground.

"Then we put your crystal in the Turnip," she said to Buzz.

"And finish the mission," Buzz added. He felt a rush of hope. Izzy's confidence was a mirror of her grandmother's. "It's a good plan."

Instinctively, Buzz held out his finger. "To infinity . . ."

But instead of tapping his finger back, Izzy looked at it, bewildered.

"Are you trying to get me to pull your finger?" she asked, suspicious.

"Don't fall for it," the taller soldier warned.

Buzz shook his head. "No, not like that. It was—sorry. It's just a thing your grandma and I used to do."

Izzy pulled a face.

"Ew," the shorter soldier said.

"I . . . we would never . . . she didn't mean to—" Buzz said, flustered. "Anyway, forget it. Moving on."

Buzz regained his composure and strode over to the Armadillo ship. "Let's load these munitions into the Armadillo and steel ourselves for combat."

Izzy pumped her fist in the air. "Operation Surprise Party is on!"

Just then, Sox's little robotic ears began to spin. "Buzz, do you hear that?"

Everyone stopped and held their breath, listening.

"I hear something," Buzz whispered. "You think it's a robot?"

"No," replied the taller soldier, "we've never seen a robot this far from the base."

Izzy cocked her head. "I don't hear anything."

Suddenly, a robot arm burst through the outpost wall.

"Oh, *now* I do!" Izzy cried.

Before Buzz could defend himself, the robot grabbed hold of Buzz's waist and pulled him through the wall, flinging him to the ground. Buzz's blaster went flying, just out of reach. He scrambled for it, but the robot's heavy, mechanical footsteps were upon him before he had a chance. The bot picked Buzz up by a leg as though he weighed nothing, holding him upside down. Then it reached for a disc on its chest plate that had the same round red button as the one that had teleported the XL-15 away.

Buzz lashed out at his captor with his free leg, and the toe of his boot connected with the disc on the robot's chest plate, knocking it loose and sending it skittering several feet away. Realizing what had happened, the robot turned and began marching toward the fallen transport disc while Buzz hung helpless in its grasp.

"Don't worry, we got you!" Izzy cried to Buzz.

"Meow!" Sox added.

The team climbed through the hole in the fort wall.

POP!

Something struck the robot! Buzz looked up, his vision swimming from all the blood rushing to his head. The bot was covered in what looked like green paint.

Several yards away, Izzy held a bazooka-like weapon. Next to her was a crate with the words TRAINING AMMO clearly stenciled on the side.

"What? Ugh," Izzy groaned. Then she called back to Buzz, "Fear not! The Junior Patrol has your back!"

"The Junior . . . *what?*" Buzz exclaimed.

Izzy fired another paintball round at the bot while she scrambled back to the box of live ammo. The shot knocked the robot's shoulder plate off, revealing some wiring. The robot extended its arm toward Izzy and fired a laser blast directly at her. Izzy ducked out of harm's way just in time—but the blast hit the Armadillo instead. The ship exploded!

"No! The ship!" Buzz cried.

The robot turned back toward the disc on the ground. Suddenly, out of nowhere, Sox pounced on the robot's head.

"Meow, meow, meow!" the little cat yowled, gouging deep scratches into the bot's single laser eye. Disoriented, it stumbled back, just as a harpoon came whizzing past and sank deep into a tree trunk behind it.

Buzz winced. The harpoon hadn't hit the bot, but it had come within millimeters of hitting *him*!

"Did I get it?" the taller soldier called, removing his helmet.

"Pretty close!" Izzy called out encouragingly.

"Sorry, I've not trained with this weapon," said the soldier. "Let me reload it!"

"Not trained?" Buzz exclaimed, his deepest fear coming true. There was no mistaking the frightened and slightly bewildered face of the lanky soldier who

had removed his helmet. A rookie, if Buzz had ever seen one. "What do you mean you're not trained?"

Meanwhile, the bot grabbed Sox by the tail and flung the cat off its face. In doing so, the robot tore some of its exposed shoulder wiring. The sparks didn't escape Buzz's notice. If he could shoot off the bot's arm, he could wriggle free.

Buzz's blaster was still out of reach on the ground. But the shorter soldier was near enough to get it.

"You, there! Grab it!" Buzz cried frantically. "Grab it!"

"Grab what?" the soldier asked, bending to see what Buzz was pointing to. She took off her helmet, revealing an old woman with weathered skin and disheveled gray hair. "Oh, no. I'm not allowed to handle weapons." She held up her hands when she realized Buzz was pointing to his blaster. "That would be a violation of my parole."

"Parole?" Buzz cried incredulously.

As if on cue, Izzy came skidding up and snatched the weapon from the ground. Buzz sucked in a breath. They had one chance.

"Izzy, now!" Buzz cried.

She swiftly threw the blaster. Izzy aimed for Buzz's left hand . . . while Buzz was reaching out expectantly with his right. The blaster went sailing by, landing somewhere in the thicket.

"Huh? No!" Buzz wailed.

"Okay, new plan!" Izzy shouted.

"New plan?" Buzz exclaimed. "What was the old plan?" He couldn't believe what was happening. He was locked in battle against a hostile alien robot, with three *rookies* as his team. Rookies, the one thing a Space Ranger couldn't count on to do anything except be reckless and unpredictable.

Buzz was going to have to take care of it himself. With a burst of effort, he crunched from his upside-down position to grab the bot's exposed wiring, and managed to rip a bolt loose before the bot shook him back down. But he'd done it—the bot's arm slumped a bit more.

Another harpoon came whizzing by, missing Buzz's head by a hair. The harpoon hit the transport disc, and in a flash of light, both it and harpoon vanished.

"Did I get it?" the taller soldier shouted.

"A little to the left!" Izzy instructed.

Buzz grunted. Mustering superhuman strength, he crunched up again and tore the remaining bolt from the bot's shoulder plate. The wiring sizzled and popped as the arm came loose, firing its laser ray wildly, now that it was disconnected from its main controls. Buzz tumbled down once he was free from the robot's grasp.

The robot thundered toward the Space Ranger as Buzz scrambled to grab the severed robotic arm.

"Ha-ha!" Buzz laughed triumphantly, swinging the arm around to fire the robot's own laser at itself. But just as Buzz took aim, the laser fizzled and died, out of power.

"What?" Buzz stammered. The robot clenched Buzz's ankle with its good hand, lifting him from the ground.

THUNK!

The robot fritzed, sputtering out a garbled *"Bzzzrrrrg. Bzzzrrrrg. Bzzzrrrrg."* Then it collapsed to the ground in a listless heap. Buzz wrested his ankle free and stared at the deactivated bot in surprise. Sticking out from its neck was a harpoon.

The taller soldier cupped a hand to his mouth like a makeshift megaphone. *"Now* did I get it?"

Chapter 9

"What—exactly—" a disheveled Buzz stammered as he paced in front of the smoldering wreckage of the Armadillo. "How did that . . . who *are* you?"

Izzy stood and saluted. "We're the Junior Patrol. At your service."

"I'm gonna need more information," Buzz said.

"We're a volunteer team of self-motivated cadets," explained Izzy. "We train one weekend a month here at the outpost. Mo and Darby"—she pointed at the taller, lanky soldier and the shorter, old woman soldier—"and I were the first to arrive last weekend, when the robots showed up. So . . . we cooked up Operation Surprise Party."

Buzz sighed. "So you're rookies?"

"Oh, boy," said Izzy. "We'd love to be rookies. Still building up to that."

Buzz couldn't believe this was happening. Just

when he thought he had some luck working with an elite squad, they turned out to be a bunch of rookies—*volunteer* rookies at that!

"Do you have munitions training?" Buzz asked.

"Partial," Izzy replied.

"Tactical engagement?"

"Pending."

"Combat experience?"

"Yes!" Izzy pointed enthusiastically at Buzz. "If you count the robot situation we just went through."

Buzz took a deep breath. These rookies seemed nice enough, and Izzy was clearly eager to live up to her grandma's legacy. But they were no replacement for trained and battle-tested Space Rangers.

He headed over to the ammo crates and began loading gear into a rover that hadn't been damaged in the attack.

"What are you doing?" Izzy asked.

"Look, you seem like nice people." Buzz heaved a harpoon gun into the rover. "I'm very supportive of your training initiatives. But I'm gonna go ahead and take it from here."

"We just saved you from that robot!" Izzy insisted.

"Excuse me?" Buzz said.

"Mo made the kill shot!"

"Mo got lucky."

Mo nodded. "Very."

Buzz closed the rover door. "So . . . if you could just point me in the direction of another ship . . ."

"Oh, they have some old ships at the abandoned storage depot," Mo said.

"Great," Buzz replied. He paused. "Where's that?"

"Oh, you can't miss it. It's over near the resource-reconstituting center," Izzy said.

Buzz shook his head. "And where's that?"

"You know, right by where the old fabrication plant used to be," Darby explained.

Buzz stared at the three of them blankly.

"What *do* you know?" Izzy asked.

"I know the base," Buzz said.

A smile crossed Izzy's face that reminded Buzz of the times when Alisha had him cornered into doing something her way. "We'll just show you," she said.

A little while later, the team's rover rumbled up to the abandoned storage depot. Buzz had never been to this part of T'Kani Prime before. He hadn't really been anywhere on T'Kani Prime outside the base and his living quarters.

He'd learned more about this team of rookies on the way. Darby had spent time in a correctional facility until she had been released on parole. She was mum about what had gotten her into jail in the first place, but she had let slip that she could take any three things and make them explode.

Mo was more of an enigma, even to himself. He'd held lots of odd jobs and couldn't seem to decide what to do with his life, so he'd signed up for the Junior Patrol on a lark. In his own words, he'd instantly regretted it.

And as for Izzy, she was obviously Alisha's grand-daughter. Maybe with time she could cut it as a Space Ranger. But now wasn't that time—not when so much was at stake.

"We can help you," Izzy insisted as Buzz unloaded the ammo and fuel crystal from the rover onto a rusted rolling cart he'd found tipped over just outside the depot.

"I appreciate that," Buzz told her. "Just go back to your training facility. Stay alert. Stay safe." He pointed to the Armadillo inside the depot. "I'm going to commandeer this P-thirty-two Armadillo and go blow up the Zurg ship."

"So, this is just goodbye?" Izzy asked, the disappointment in her voice clear.

"Affirmative." Buzz nodded. "Goodbye." Then he pushed the squeaking cart carrying the supplies and Sox into the building, leaving the Junior Patrol behind.

The storage depot had obviously been out of use for some time. Inside, it was dark and creepy, with only an occasional shaft of light filtering in through the filmy skylights above. Buzz looked up and recoiled in disgust. The building's rafters were filled with rows and rows of enormous chrysalises. Sox scanned them, revealing thermal signals.

"Life forms detected," he told Buzz.

"What are they?" Buzz asked.

"Giant insectoid organisms," Sox confirmed. "This building appears to be some sort of hive."

Buzz took in the thousands of chrysalises drooping from the rafters and felt his skin crawl. "Are they a threat?"

"Sensors indicate they are hibernating," Sox replied.

"Very good." Buzz nodded. Just then, he caught a glint of light reflecting off something white in a fenced-in locker area of the depot. His eyes grew wide. "Whoa. . . ."

"What is it?" Sox asked.

"I'll show you," Buzz said. He hurriedly wheeled the squeaking dolly over to the locker area. On display was Buzz's old Space Ranger suit, alongside three others. There was no mistaking the name badge on the suit: LIGHTYEAR. It was his! The thrill of seeing that suit again was like jumping into a time portal. Buzz didn't waste a second in putting it on. He struck a few poses, reveling in its comfort and familiarity.

He turned and saw Izzy, Mo, and Darby standing there.

"Sorry to interrupt," Izzy said. "Looks like you were having a real nice moment."

"What are you doing here?" Buzz hissed, eyeing the sleeping insects up above. "It's not safe!"

"You took the keys to our truck," Darby said.

"Oh, there they are!" Mo spotted them on the dolly. He went to grab the keys, but accidentally knocked them off the cart, causing them to hit the floor and trigger the truck's alarm outside. Flashing lights and the honking horn reverberated around the depot.

"Shhh, quiet!" Buzz warned as Mo fumbled with the key fob.

Mo finally turned off the alarm, but it was too late. The bugs were already stirring from their sleep. Two chrysalises cracked down the center. Insect appendages reached out grotesquely, ripping the cocoons in half. Two of the most hideous, stomach-turning insects Buzz had ever seen emerged from the chrysalises. They spotted the team and shrieked, awakening their hibernating siblings.

CRACK. CRACK. CRACK.

One by one, all the chrysalises began to split open, revealing thousands of alien insects.

Chapter 10

In a horrific swarm, the insects descended on the team!

"Somebody get the door!" Buzz and Izzy shouted in unison.

Scrambling, the team rushed forward and slammed the locker-area gate closed just in time. The bugs angrily clawed at the fence, their appendages reaching through the bars.

"Well, I'm going to be blunt here," Mo said. "I wish that hadn't happened."

"So do the rest of us!" Darby snapped.

"Everyone grab a weapon!" Buzz ordered, tossing the team blasters from the ammo cart.

"Boy, I'd love to," Darby said. "But my parole—"

"As a Star Command officer, I grant you authority," Buzz directed. "We're going to blast our way out of here."

Darby smiled and grabbed a weapon. "Now we're talking."

"Buzz," Sox said seriously, "the probability of surviving a frontal attack is only thirty-eight point two percent."

"Seems a bit low," said Mo.

"Oh! What about stealth mode?" said Izzy, pointing to a button on Buzz's chest plate.

"How do you know about stealth mode?" Buzz asked, surprised.

"Grandma and I used to play stealth mode all the time," Izzy explained. "It was like hide-and-seek, but with a twist."

"Okay, well, it's actually good thinking," Buzz said. "I'll use stealth mode to disorient them."

Izzy pointed at the other three Space Ranger suits. "Or . . . and stick with me here. We could *all* use stealth mode and just walk right out."

Buzz hesitated. Not just anyone could wear a Space Ranger suit.

Izzy showed him a nameplate on one of the suits. "This one even has my name on it!"

Despite himself, Buzz was impressed. It was a good plan. Everyone would use stealth mode. Buzz and Sox would head to the Armadillo, and the rest of the group would go in the opposite direction, toward the truck.

A few minutes later, the team of four stood suited up and at the ready.

"Check it out! I'm Feathers . . . Featherin . . . Featherinsham . . . ," said Mo, trying to read the long name. He noticed a small pen tucked into the chest plate of the suit. "Oh, look! A pen! Cool! Does yours have a pen?"

"Okay, pay attention," Buzz instructed. "Stealth mode is fairly simple. There are just two parts. You press the button—"

"Is it this button?" Mo interrupted, pointing to a bright red button on his suit.

"I will tell you which button," Buzz said.

"What does this button do?" Mo pointed to a shiny blue button instead.

Buzz waved Mo's question away. "I'm sorry, we're not going to have time to go over all the buttons."

"Okay, what about this thing?" Mo reached for a red pull tab on the side of his suit.

"No!" Buzz grabbed his hand. *That's* the surrender string. You never pull that."

"There is no more shameful maneuver for a Space Ranger," Izzy said seriously.

"Excuse me, did I miss *which* button is the stealth mode button?" Darby asked, annoyed.

"You push *this* button!" Frustrated, Buzz jabbed his finger at a bright green button on the chest plate.

"But *not* yet!" He grabbed Mo's hand again just as the cadet's finger hovered over the button. "You push *this* button, then *you* go out the front door, and *I'll* go blow up the Zurg ship. Ready?"

"Ready," the Junior Patrol replied in unison.

"Okay. Goodbye—again." Buzz motioned for them to all press their buttons. Together, they faded from view.

While the Junior Patrol crept toward the entrance, Buzz wheeled the ammo cart to the Armadillo, avoiding crawling insects along the way. Sox was crammed into Buzz's helmet.

"Sox, you're inhibiting my visual," Buzz said, spitting fur out of his mouth.

Sox shifted slightly. "Is this better?"

"Negative," Buzz replied.

Buzz placed Sox on his shoulder, making Sox appear to float in midair along with the cart that seemed to be rolling on its own. None of the bugs paid them any attention.

"Very good," Buzz whispered to himself. "Stealth mode is working as planned."

He loaded the ammo and inserted the glowing fuel crystal into the Armadillo with a satisfying click. Then he checked the stealth mode countdown on his wrist display. He still had ten seconds left before stealth mode ran out and he was visible again. He hopped into the Armadillo just as the countdown ended and his stealth-mode bubble fizzled out.

Then he gasped. "Wait—the timer! They don't know about the timer!"

Panicked, Buzz looked out the hatch door to where Izzy, Mo, and Darby were only halfway toward the depot exit—in full view!

The Junior Patrol realized they were visible at the same time the bugs did. With blood-curdling shrieks, the insects crawled toward them!

"I surrender!" Mo cried, yanking the red surrender string on his suit. It inflated like a giant raspberry.

Izzy and Darby tried to roll Mo toward the exit, but it was blocked by a legion of bugs. With a yelp, they turned around and started pushing him toward the Armadillo. The army of bugs followed.

"No, no!" Buzz yelled. "Do *not* approach the vehicle!"

Before Buzz could stop them, Izzy and Darby rolled Mo right up to the ship—except his suit was too wide to fit through the Armadillo door! Thinking fast, Buzz reached in and pulled the release on Mo's suit, deflating it to its normal size. The Junior Patrol toppled in just as Buzz slammed the door closed. The insects screamed angrily, scraping at the hull.

"All right!" Izzy panted. "Way to adapt, team!"

"Why are you congratulating yourselves?" Buzz asked incredulously.

"Because I Hawthorned us right out of that situation!" Izzy exclaimed.

Buzz couldn't hide his frustration. "But you could have made it if—"

"If you had *told* us stealth mode wears off," Mo said, still shaken.

Buzz wanted to snap back, but in a rare moment, he realized he didn't have a retort. The cadet was right. How could they know about the stealth mode timer if Buzz hadn't told them?

Suddenly, the ship lurched. The insects had swarmed it, covering the hull and windshield, rocking it back and forth. There wasn't any time left.

"Okay, everyone just strap in!" Buzz commanded. It looked like they were going to bust out of here the old-fashioned way.

Buzz powered up the ship.

The navigation system chimed to life. "Hello. I am—"

Buzz slammed IVAN off and engaged the thrusters. With a belabored metallic groan, the ship lifted off the floor and rose toward the ceiling, shattering through the skylights.

"Hold on!" Buzz ordered, pushing the throttle.

Several alien bugs still clung to the hull trying to tear their way in, even as the ship blasted higher into the atmosphere.

"Are . . . are we going into space?" Izzy stammered from the seat behind him. Her voice sounded strange.

"No, I'm going to drop you somewhere," Buzz told her. But as he barrel-rolled the ship to shake the remaining bugs loose, they crossed the threshold of the atmosphere just enough to see stars.

"I can see stars!" Izzy yelped in terror. "That *is* space!"

Buzz looked over his shoulder at her. "What is happening right now?"

"She's afraid of space," Darby said bluntly.

"What!" Buzz exclaimed.

"Look out! A ship!" Izzy cried.

Buzz turned back just in time to see a fighter ship directly in front of them. It was on an intercept course—and it was opening fire!

Chapter 11

"What is that?" Buzz cried, swerving to avoid the enemy ship's blasters.

He rolled the Armadillo, narrowly escaping the first three blasts. But the fourth shot clipped the right wing of their ship, and they plummeted back toward the ground.

"I can't see anything!" Buzz cried as they passed from gray skies into sudden darkness.

"Oh, no!" exclaimed Izzy. "We're on the dark side of the planet!"

Sox spun his head around, scanning the area. He stopped, eyes wide. "Oh! Over there! Ten o'clock!"

Buzz saw the faint glow of lights and fires from a mining operation in the distance.

"Hold on!" he shouted, gripping the control wheel. "This isn't going to be pretty!"

Mustering all the control he had, Buzz steadily

held the wheel and guided the flailing ship down to the ground, even though he knew it was going to be a rough landing.

FWA-BOOM!

The ship slammed into the terrain, and in a plume of dust, it came to a rest.

"Is everyone okay?" Buzz winced as he started to move his body.

"I think so." Izzy sat up, winded.

The others nodded, dazed but unharmed.

Buzz snapped his attention back to the windshield, looking for signs of the enemy ship that had shot them down. He couldn't see anything—it was pitch black out there.

He clamored to the door and opened it with a *whoosh*. Thankfully, there was no sign of the fighter ship anywhere. But their ship didn't look to be in very good shape.

"Sox, get me a damage report," he said.

"One moment, please," Sox said. *"Beep boop beep boop beep boop . . ."*

Meanwhile, Izzy knelt on the ground, taking deep breaths. "Okay," she panted. "This is better."

Buzz stared at her, all his frustration bubbling over. "*This* is better?"

"No, obviously this is worse overall," Izzy conceded.

"I just meant—you know." She pointed up toward the stars.

Buzz clutched his head. "Wait, *how* are you afraid of space?"

"Oh, it's pretty easy," Izzy explained. "Did you know if you let go out there, you just keep going in the same direction? Forever. Just . . ." She made a whooshing sound and pantomimed floating off into space.

"Then how were you going to blow up the Zurg ship?" Buzz pressed.

"Oh, I would have been ground support." Izzy shrugged, embarrassed. "I know Grandma wasn't afraid of space."

"No, because she was a *Space* Ranger. Astrophobia is an automatic disqualification!"

Izzy looked down at the ground, and Buzz softened a little. He didn't want to hurt the kid's feelings. But there was a difference between pretending to be a Space Ranger and actually *being* a Space Ranger. Facing your fears head-on and having the courage to conquer them was a crucial component of joining the Space Ranger Corps. It was one of the first things Alisha had taught him—something she had understood even better than Buzz.

"What was that thing?" Darby asked, breaking the tension. She squinted up into the dark sky.

Buzz shook his head. "I don't know." Then he plodded over to the ship and removed the fuel crystal. It was unharmed, glowing with its ever-steady shimmery colors. But now they were all stranded. Again. With a broken ship and hostile forces surrounding them. No matter what he did, Buzz couldn't catch a break. No matter how hard he tried, he couldn't seem to make things right. At every turn there was a roadblock, and then another, and another.

"I was done," he said, allowing himself to wallow in self-pity for just a moment, which was something Alisha had always discouraged. "I finally had the crystal. This was supposed to be over." He groaned. "But who am I kidding? I don't need a crystal. I need a time machine to get out of this mess."

Just then, Sox snapped back to reality. "*Bing!* Assessment complete."

"How bad is it?" Buzz asked, figuring he already knew the answer.

"The blast was absorbed by the heat shield," Sox explained. "It only caused a minor electrical short."

"Okay . . . ," Buzz said, unsure if this was a good thing or a bad thing.

"So in order to be flight operational," Sox continued, "the Armadillo will require material of specialized capacitance."

"Oh! Like an electrical thingy," Mo replied.

"How do you know that?" Darby asked.

"We learned this," Mo said. "Specialized capacitance? Remember? We built those field radios last month."

"Oh, yeah," said Izzy. "That was fun."

"Yeah, Darby messed hers up," Mo chuckled.

"I'm gonna mess *you* up," Darby grumbled.

Meanwhile, Buzz was analyzing the ship's engine. He turned to the group, annoyed. "Please, I'm trying to think here."

But the Junior Patrol continued bickering about their radios.

"Hey!" Buzz interjected. "Honestly . . . there is a lot of room out here. If you want to reminisce, you can go . . . over there!" Buzz pointed to the distance. "Or, look! There's no one trying to think over there." He gestured again to another area.

Izzy pointed to the mining facility, which was glowing in the distance. "We can go up there!"

"Fine. Perfect," Buzz said, waving them away.

"Okay, new plan!" Izzy nodded.

"Wait, what?" Buzz said.

"That mining facility will have a console, right?" said Izzy. "That console will have a little coil thing, right? And that little coil thing will have the . . ." She pointed at Mo.

"Specialized capacitance," Mo finished.

"Huh," Buzz said. Despite his earlier frustration, he couldn't help feeling a tiny bit proud of Izzy for figuring a way out of their predicament. "Now that's thinking like a Hawthorne," he told her. "Let's go get that part and get out of here . . . before that thing finds us again."

Together, the team trekked over the rocky terrain that led to the mining operation. When they reached the top of a ravine overlooking the entire enterprise, Buzz whistled. The mine was massive—a gigantic crater dug deep into the planet's surface, where, far below, mining robots had excavated resources from T'Kani Prime's crust. A command-center building stood several yards away, extending precariously over the ravine ledge and held in place by giant metal stilts. Darby was the first to reach the door, but it was sealed tight. She fumbled with something in her pocket while Buzz spoke into his wrist recorder.

"Buzz Lightyear, mission log," he narrated out of habit. "In order to repair our ship, we have to find some way to get inside this command center, and—"

Just then, the door slid open. Darby stood, satisfied, holding a lockpick she'd used to hot-wire the control system.

"Oh," Buzz said, surprised. "Nice job, elderly convict."

Quickly, they slipped inside the command center

and slid the door shut behind them. It was dark inside the control room, which was lit only by emergency lights. Normally, operators from Star Command would be on duty there, but they were all trapped back at the base.

"Okay, the activation coil should be in here," Izzy said, pointing to a large control console nearby.

Sox shimmied underneath it.

Mo pulled out the pen from his suit. "Oh! Need a pen?"

Sox didn't respond. All everyone heard was the sound of an electric screwdriver.

"And . . . got it!" Sox shouted triumphantly as he emerged holding the activation coil in his mouth.

"Okay, yeah. Another time," said Mo.

As Mo pocketed the pen, his elbow hit a large red button on a wall.

"Security measures activated," a robotic voice announced.

Warning lights flashed, and before the group could react, the door to the control room sealed shut. Force fields shot down from the ceiling, surrounding each of them in individual energy cones.

"No! Not again!" Darby exclaimed.

"Not *what*? What is this?" Buzz cried.

He pushed against his force field and it moved along with him. He was trapped inside!

"It holds you until *they* come and get you," said Darby.

"Well, no one is coming to get us," Mo argued. "They're all trapped in the base. So we should just leave, right?"

"We can't just leave!" Darby exclaimed.

"Sure, we can," Mo said. "Take it from me. You can always just leave."

Mo slammed his cone into the door button, and instantly, the door whizzed open again. But the energy field prevented him from passing through it.

Darby warned Mo to be careful, but Mo crashed into the closing door and collided with Darby, merging their force fields into one. They were squished uncomfortably close together inside.

"All right, sorry," said Mo. "But maybe if we both try it?"

"That's not gonna work!" Darby exclaimed.

"You haven't even tried!" Mo said.

Mo threw his body at the door button once more, but without Darby's help, they stumbled back and knocked into Izzy and Sox. Now their force fields all merged into one uncomfortably tight cone.

Squished, they turned toward Buzz.

"Stay away from me!" Buzz warned. "I'm no help to anyone if I'm stuck in there with you." He looked at the activation coil in his hand and sighed, tucking it into his pocket. One more roadblock. "Sox, can you turn these off?"

Sox clawed at the group's force field. "I can't reach the controls."

With the team squished together, even the slightest movement caused them to stagger. They accidentally bumped into a gray power source box, causing the lights and cones to flicker.

That gave Buzz an idea. "I'll open the door, you slam into the power source . . . these things will disappear, and we'll walk right out."

Everyone nodded.

"Ready?" Buzz asked. "Go!"

Buzz slammed the door button while the other four charged at the power source. The door opened upon contact, but the team's force field just bounced off the gray box. Nothing happened.

Izzy gasped. "We're just not heavy enough. Buzz, we need you!"

"Wait, in there? But if it doesn't work, I won't be able to save you," Buzz protested.

"You don't need to save us," Izzy said. "You need to *join* us."

Buzz considered her words. It did seem like the best possible option. After all, there was little he could do in his force field alone. But together, maybe there was a chance.

Squaring his shoulders, Buzz slammed into the door control button, causing the door to spring back open. He used the recoil to power his momentum toward the team's force field. As soon as they combined, they crashed into the gray box. They slammed into it again and again until it finally exploded.

The blast knocked everyone to the floor while simultaneously cutting the power. Their energy cones disappeared, and the door, which had been automatically closing, slid to a stop halfway.

Buzz shook his head—he'd hit it hard in the aftermath. In his stupor, he felt the floor of the control room shift and drop. Then he realized that the support structures holding the building over the ravine were giving way.

"Go, go!" he croaked, motioning the team toward the half-open door. Everyone scrambled to their feet and began heading for the exit, when Buzz heard a metal *clang*. He felt his pocket and turned when he discovered that it was empty. The activation coil had slipped out and was rolling along the pitch of the floor . . . toward the collapsing walls over the ravine!

Buzz sprinted toward it.

"Buzz, no!" Izzy cried when she saw what was happening.

But Buzz didn't listen. He leaped for the activation coil, his fingers closing around it just before it could fall through a hole that had crumbled away in the floor. In one smooth motion, he pivoted on his knees and sprang back up, clamoring up the tilted floor back to where his horrified crew watched. He was almost there. Fresh cracks formed under his boots as he dodged falling debris and grabbed hold of an edge of the control console to propel himself forward. The floor was practically vertical at this point. With a sickening groan, the entire room pulled away from the ledge where his friends stood, forming a chasm between him and the open door. There were only milliseconds to make a choice. Buzz leaped across the split, flying through the air. With the coil clutched firmly in one hand, he stretched his other hand out to grab hold on to the ledge. He just barely made it as the rest of the control center collapsed away. He was safe!

And then, without warning, the piece of ledge Buzz clung to broke away, too. Suddenly he was falling, dropping down toward the darkness with nothing left to grab hold of, nothing left to cling to, nothing to save him from the choice he had made—

Then Izzy's hand clasped around Buzz's wrist, abruptly halting his descent. He looked up in disbelief. The team had formed a chain, one hand to another, giving Izzy just enough length to reach down and catch him.

"We got you," she said.

Chapter 12

A short while later, the team sat together in a break room, which somehow hadn't collapsed in the destruction. They were all still stunned, Buzz most of all. He sat quietly, staring across the darkened room.

"Here, let's all recharge a little." Mo offered Buzz a sandwich he'd scrounged from the vending machine. Sox uncapped the flash drive on his tail and plugged it into a wall outlet. His eyes lit up with charging symbols.

Buzz distractedly peeled off the sandwich's wrapper. But when he felt the slimy texture, he looked down. The sandwich appeared to be several pieces of juicy meat wrapped around a piece of bread.

"What, uh—what's happening here?" he asked.

"Something wrong with your sandwich?" Izzy took a bite of her own.

"Why is the meat on the outside?" Buzz asked, completely confused.

" 'Cause it's a sandwich," Mo muttered with his mouth full.

"No," Buzz said. "The bread is supposed to be on the outside."

"What, like bread-meat-bread?" Mo asked.

"That's too much bread," Darby added.

"Yeah, but this is all . . . wet." Buzz held his sandwich up at an angle, allowing some of the juice to drip onto the floor.

"Yeah, juicy fingers," Mo nodded. "That's the best part."

"When's the last time you had a sandwich?" Izzy asked.

"I don't know," Buzz shrugged. "A hundred years ago? Give or take?"

Mo chuckled to himself. "This guy . . . bread-meat-bread."

"It's too much bread," Darby repeated. "That would just suck all the moisture out of your mouth."

Mo laughed and accidentally kicked Sox loose from the outlet. Sox's eyes faded away to darkness.

"Oh, no, Sox!" Mo cried.

The team rushed over to the robotic cat. After a moment, his eyes turned on once more. He looked at the group, disoriented.

"Excuse me," Sox said. "I require a reboot." His eyes closed and a chime began to play.

Buzz Lightyear

Captain Buzz Lightyear has the most important qualities that a Space Ranger should have: courage, independence, and, above all, determination. When he and his crew become stranded on a hostile alien planet, Buzz becomes more determined than ever to finish his mission—*his* way. But as the obstacles to his success mount, Buzz's friends begin to show him a different way of working . . . as a team.

Alisha Hawthorne

Commander Alisha Hawthorne is one of the most respected Space Rangers in the corps. She loves going on adventures, traveling amongst the stars, and teasing her best friend, Buzz, whenever she gets the chance. After she and Buzz get stranded on the planet T'Kani Prime, Alisha leads her crew on the ground in starting a new life there.

Sox

Sox is Buzz's adorable robot cat companion. Created to support Buzz after his time away, Sox makes it his own mission to be as helpful to Buzz as possible, using advanced analytics, computer programming, and an array of gadgets. But more important, this cute kitty quickly becomes a friend and sidekick Buzz can always rely on.

Izzy Hawthorne

As the granddaughter of Space Ranger Alisha Hawthorne, Izzy has always dreamed of a life of adventure and exploring the universe. Unfortunately, she is absolutely terrified of space. But to the always upbeat and determined Izzy, that is just a minor setback. She joins the Junior Patrol in hopes of getting the training she needs—maybe even from the most famous Space Ranger of all: Buzz Lightyear.

Darby Steel

Darby is the oldest member of the Junior Patrol, but don't be fooled by her age. She is tougher than most, with her no-nonsense attitude and ability to put any three things together and make them explode. As part of her prison parole program, Darby begrudgingly joins the Junior Patrol, but with her fearlessness and grit, she becomes an indispensable part of the team.

Maurice "Mo" Morrison

Mo isn't sure what he wants to do with his life, but he knows for an absolute fact that he doesn't want to die. Avoiding conflict and risk as much as possible, Mo isn't thrilled when the Junior Patrol gets involved in a high-stakes mission to save the planet from alien forces. But all Mo needs is a bit of confidence, which his team is happy to help him with.

Cal Burnside

As the new leader of Star Command, Commander Burnside is content to stay on T'Kani Prime. His pride and joy is the advanced laser shield, built to protect Star Command and all the citizens from vines, bugs, and alien invasions. Buzz Lightyear sees it differently—the laser shield is keeping everyone in!

Zurg

Zurg is the terrifying and powerful robot that has invaded T'Kani Prime. With its bloodred eyes, huge stature, and even bigger ship and robot army, Zurg is the most fearsome foe that Star Command has ever faced. This mechanical menace will stop at nothing to find Buzz Lightyear—even if it means searching the entire galaxy!

"I'm sorry," Mo said, his voice tight with emotion. "I almost killed Sox. I almost got us all killed back there."

"Hey. Listen to me," Izzy said. "It was just a mistake."

But Mo didn't seem comforted. Izzy looked to Buzz for support. "Right, Buzz?"

Buzz blinked, shaken from his thoughts. "Oh, uh." He cleared his throat. "Just . . . try to be a little better," he told Mo.

Buzz's words only made Mo's shoulders slump further. Izzy shot Buzz a look.

"Listen," Buzz continued. "When I first went to the academy, I was not . . . you know . . . good. I screwed up. Every day. I got tangled in the obstacle course. My hands shook so much, I couldn't hit the target. Not the bull's-eye, the *whole* target. And I was going to quit after the first week. It was clear I was *not* Space Ranger material."

Mo looked up at Buzz. "Really?"

"Yeah," said Buzz, "but Commander Hawthorne saw something in me. So I started looking for it, too."

Just then, Sox opened his eyes. "Recalibrating. One corrupted file restored."

He began to show a hologram of Alisha.

"Hey, he's lighting up!" Alisha exclaimed in the hologram. "It's working." She turned to Sox. "Hello,

93

Sox. I need you to look after my best friend." She held up a photo of Buzz. "His name is Buzz. He's away right now, but he'll be back soon. He's going to save us."

The message ended, and the group was quiet. Buzz walked over to the edge of the room, looking at the mine below.

"What's wrong?" Izzy asked.

"*What's wrong?*" Buzz repeated. "Did you not hear that? She believed I could fix the mistake I made. And that belief cost her everything."

"Everything?" Izzy said incredulously. "No. She had Grandma Kiko, my dad and me, all her friends. She didn't plan to be here, but she had a whole life on this planet, Buzz. All of us have." She paused. "Except . . . for you."

Buzz shook his head. "Yeah, but we wanted to be Space Rangers again. We wanted to *matter*."

Izzy looked Buzz in the eye, and her expression suddenly seemed much older. "Believe me . . . she mattered."

For a moment, Buzz could swear he heard Alisha's voice in Izzy's. Maybe he had been thinking about this all wrong.

He absentmindedly took a bite of his juicy sandwich and tilted his head. "You know, it is pretty good this way."

"Yeah," Izzy said. "Bread-meat-bread . . . how long did you do it like that?"

"Forever," Buzz admitted, making everyone smile. And this time, their smiles didn't fade.

Ba-ding!

The team looked over at Sox as he unplugged himself from the wall.

"Fully recharged," Sox confirmed.

"Come on," Buzz said. "Let's go put this part in the ship and get out of here."

As the team walked out of the command center, Sox turned on his flashlight mode, leading them through the darkness.

"This is exciting," Izzy said. "Operation Surprise Party, here we come!"

Buzz looked at her, confused. "Negative. I can't put you in harm's way like that."

"What, are you going to do the whole mission alone?" Izzy protested.

"I can do it," Buzz said confidently.

"Because you have a Hawthorne right here!" Izzy pointed at herself.

Buzz couldn't help smiling. Izzy really had inherited her grandmother's gumption. Maybe that was why it was even more important to him now to keep her safe. He saw so much of his old friend in Izzy.

And he didn't want to fail Alisha again by putting her granddaughter in danger.

"I appreciate that," he said. "And I'll let you know if I need you. Until then, let's just try to get back to the Armadillo without any more trouble."

Suddenly, a giant explosion erupted in the rock face behind them. The team was knocked off their feet, strewn about the ground like rag dolls.

Buzz coughed and peered through the dust. Standing ominously in the aftermath of the explosion was another robot. But this one was different. It was humongous, constructed out of shimmering purple metal, its bloodred eyes glowing viciously beneath a silver horned crown.

"Run!" Buzz cried to the team.

Everyone clambered to their feet in the chaos, trying to find an escape route. But Mo crashed into Darby and the two toppled to the ground, snagging Sox in the fray. Izzy, who had been following closely behind Buzz, turned and gasped. She sprinted back to help her friends.

When Buzz realized the others weren't behind him, he skidded to a halt and spun around. His heart dropped. All of them—Mo, Darby, Izzy, and Sox—were tangled in a heap several yards back. And the robot loomed over them. There no escape now.

"No!" Buzz cried in despair as the robot lifted a massive foot, ready to crush the rookies like bugs.

Izzy and her friends cowered, bracing for the end.

The robot's foot lowered . . . and passed right over them. The bot marched on, leaving the team untouched, heading straight for the Space Ranger.

"What?" Buzz whispered, backing away. He looked at his team, then back at the advancing robot. And his eyes grew wide with a cold rush of clarity.

"It's after me . . . ," Buzz said, realizing. He urgently waved his team toward the ship. "Go!" he yelled. "Go back to the ship!"

"But, Buzz!" he heard Izzy cry after him as he leaped back down into the mining canyon. He had to lead that robot away—it was the only way to save his friends.

He slipped and skidded down a steep embankment and darted into a tunnel. Charging at full speed, he curved around a bend, following a soft glow of light that guided the way toward another exit. But just as he got there, the robot's shadow loomed large. It blocked the exit with a metal rebar, stopping Buzz in his tracks. The Space Ranger pivoted and ran back in the other direction. To his left was a small crevice between two rock faces. Buzz slipped inside, hoping to hide. But the robot smashed the entire wall to pieces, sending Buzz fleeing once more.

No matter where Buzz ran, the robot always seemed to be two steps ahead of him. It was like it knew his every move. Buzz sprinted down a large storage passage, past rows of deactivated plasma drills . . . and came to a dead end. The robot's shadow crept over him. He was trapped.

Buzz whirled, bracing for a fight. The robot pointed its blaster at him.

"Buzz . . . ," the robot said in a deep mechanical voice.

"What?" Buzz panted hard. "How do you know my name?"

The robot's blaster retracted inside its metallic arm, and was replaced by a robotic hand. "Come with me."

"What?" Buzz stared in total confusion.

BOOM!

Buzz jumped back, shocked. The plasma drill next to him had powered up and blasted the robot in the chest. It was knocked offline! Buzz stared in disbelief as three figures and a little robotic cat revealed themselves from behind the plasma drill.

Darby chuckled. "This is *definitely* a violation of my parole." Then she aimed the plasma drill at the wall and fired again, creating an escape route back to the surface.

"Come on!" Izzy yelled. "Let's get out of here!"

Moving as one, the team bounded out of the tunnel, up and over the ravine ledge, and slid down the hillside toward the Armadillo.

In the dark sky above, pinpoints of light grew large. It was a legion of enemy ships descending toward their location. A battle was imminent.

Everyone raced aboard the Armadillo and strapped in.

"Ready yourselves for launch!" Buzz directed them. "Operation Surprise Party is back on!"

"What? With us?" Izzy exclaimed, excitement and terror comingling in her voice.

Buzz looked back at the Junior Patrol with new admiration. They had saved him not just once, but twice. And besides, there was no safe place to take them anymore—not with a barrage of enemy vessels en route and locked on target. In space or on the ground, every place was dangerous. They were better off facing the danger together as a team.

Buzz bantered with them, the way he used to with Alisha. "What, am I going to do the whole mission alone?"

"We can't launch yet," Sox reminded him. "I still need five minutes to install the coil."

"We can't sit here for five minutes!" Darby cried desperately as she watched an army of robots emerging from their pods.

"The ship still has hover capabilities," said Sox.

"Then let's use them!" Buzz exclaimed.

He punched the hover throttle, and the ship began zipping just above the ground, dodging enemy robots left and right.

"We might lose them in the fire geysers," Izzy suggested.

"Point the way," Buzz agreed. He turned to Darby and Mo. "You two, blast some robots!"

Darby smiled and opened the weapon cases.

"But we haven't even finished our munitions training," Mo whispered to Darby.

"Shhh!" said Darby. "How hard can it be? Look. We got these spiky things, and these ones probably explode. Just do whatever feels right."

"What?" said Mo skeptically. "What are *you* going to do?"

Darby hoisted a bazooka onto her shoulder with satisfaction. "I'm gonna dance with Mr. Boom."

She moved to the back door of the ship and kicked it open. As a robot flew toward the door, Darby fired the bazooka and blasted it away.

Explosions lit the dark side of the planet like fireworks. One by one, the robots dropped as Mo and Darby hit their targets. Some accidentally activated their own transport discs upon impact, causing them to vanish into thin air. Surprisingly, none of the robots seemed to be retaliating with firepower. Instead, they steadily swarmed the ship, each attempting to attach a transport disc to the hull.

Meanwhile, the bubbling lava of the fire pits loomed dead ahead.

"Don't worry," Izzy told Buzz. "I know every last inch of—watch out!" She pointed at a stalagmite just in time. The Armadillo clipped it, sending a chunk of rock into a pursuing robot.

"Repair fifty-percent complete," Sox announced.

"Left!" Izzy yelled to Buzz. He did as she directed, narrowly missing a blazing geyser of fire that caught an unsuspecting robot in the blast.

"Here we go," Buzz said. He pushed the throttle forward, and they flew across the molten terrain.

A dozen more robots zoomed toward the Armadillo, closing in fast. Darby rained lasers upon them, blasting them down into the bubbling lava— all except one. It managed to evade her long enough to reach the hull and slap a transport disc on the side.

"Quick! Give me something!" Buzz shouted to Darby.

He reached his arm back, and Darby swiftly fastened a white laser gauntlet she found onto his wrist. He slammed a button to open the side window and blasted the alien robot away. The Armadillo sailed forward, free and clear of the lava pits, and back over stable terrain.

"Ninety-percent complete!" Sox announced.

"Izzy." Buzz turned and locked eyes with her. "Do you know how to transfer power on the fly?"

"I've done it in the simulator," Izzy said, a little uncertain.

Buzz threw a few switches. "Well, it's about to get real. Ready, thrusters!"

Izzy searched the console, doubt clouding her expression.

"Green button," Buzz said, guiding her.

Izzy found it and pressed it hard. "Done!"

Meanwhile, a robot was closing in on the ship. Darby tried to line up her shot, but it kept swerving back and forth, evading her.

"Ninety-nine percent complete!" Sox called.

"Izzy, transfer to—"

"Oscillating power!" Izzy completed Buzz's thought, pushing the correct button. "Done!"

The robot was getting closer, its transport disc outstretched. Darby squinted through her weapon's scope. She had the robot in her crosshairs.

"One-hundred percent complete!" Sox announced. The repair was finished!

"Okay, not yet . . . ," Buzz said to Izzy as he watched a gauge on the dash.

Izzy's hand hovered nervously over the console, close to the buttons.

"Fuel check!" Buzz called.

"Fuel eject!" Izzy replied.

Suddenly, with a sickening lurch, the Armadillo ground to a halt, dropping unceremoniously to the planet's surface. Darby was knocked off-balance and fired her shot into dead air while the tracking bot zipped past. The dashboard flashed a warning: FUEL CELL EJECT.

Izzy looked at Buzz, her heart sinking. "Oh, no."

Buzz hurried to the window and spied the ship's fuel cell lying on the ground outside.

"Blast!" he cried.

Buzz kicked open the side door, and he and Izzy sprinted across the rocky terrain to where the fuel cell lay. The robot that had been tailing them bore down, heading for it as well. Buzz aimed his wrist blaster.

"Grab the crystal!" he yelled to Izzy.

Buzz fired at the robot, blowing off its arm. But the robot sailed over him, heading straight for the glowing fuel source.

Buzz turned to aim again, but the bot was in front of Izzy now. He didn't have a clear shot. Izzy dove for the crystal just as the bot snatched it up.

"No!" she cried.

Immediately, the robot pressed its transport disc and vanished. It was gone. And so was the fuel crystal.

"No," Buzz groaned, sinking to his knees.

He couldn't believe it. Without the crystal, they had nothing. No way to reach the Zurg ship. No way to get it back. That fuel crystal had been their only hope. And just like that, the mission was over.

"Buzz?" Izzy said, her voice near tears as she walked over to him. "I'm so sorry. Everything was happening so fast, and I just—I made a mistake."

Buzz looked at her. He wasn't even sure what he felt right now.

"Yeah," he said, defeated.

Izzy looked crestfallen. "But we're not done. We can still do something, right?"

"Izzy, look around!" Buzz spread his arms out over the vast wasteland. "There's nothing *to* do. The mission . . . it's over."

Saying that out loud was like a punch to the gut. Accepting defeat was something Buzz had never done before. Something he'd never allowed himself to do. But he had failed in every sense of the word. He had let down his old team. He had been wrong to trust a band of volunteer rookies to help him. The culmination of everything he had dedicated his life and others' lives to meant nothing now.

Buzz slowly got up and started to walk away.

"Buzz?" Izzy asked, frightened. "Buzz! Where are you going?"

"I just need to . . . be by myself," Buzz said.

He plodded forward, dust billowing under his footsteps as the rest of the team watched, heartbroken.

That was when something grabbed Buzz through the darkness. It was a giant mechanical hand, extending from the robot cloaked in shining purple metal. The robot's eyes burned fiery red.

"No!" Izzy cried.

Buzz struggled as the robot lifted him off the ground. Its eyes flashed in the direction of the team for a moment. Then it reached for a large transport disc on its chest.

"Buzz!" the team shouted.

The robot pressed the button, and they vanished.

Buzz was gone.

Chapter 13

A low mechanical hum filled the transport room, oddly serene amid the pile of deactivated robots that lay in a heap on the teleportation pad. Suddenly, there was a flash of light, and Buzz appeared—still trapped in the robot's clutches.

Straining, Buzz fired his wrist laser at the robot, taking it by surprise just long enough to wriggle free from its grasp and roll out of reach. Buzz fired his laser again, but this time, the robot just absorbed the blast, chuckling a deep, throaty noise that rumbled through its metallic chambers.

"What is this?" Buzz demanded. "Where are we? Who are you?"

The robot simply shook its head, as if denying the truth to a young child. "Everything will make sense. In due time. For now, you can call me Zurg."

"All right, *Zurg,*" Buzz said, still tracking the

menacing foe with his wrist laser. "Then tell me what you want."

"I want the same thing you want, Buzz." Zurg took a step closer. "I want to help you. I want you to finish the mission."

"This mission?" Buzz echoed, taken aback. "What do you know about the mission?"

"I know everything," Zurg said. "I know about the crash on T'Kani Prime. About the mistake *you* made. I want to help you fix it."

Buzz shook his head, confused. "That doesn't make sense—how could you know that?"

"Because *I'm* from the future," Zurg revealed. "Where the machinery is so advanced, it can do anything, even travel through time. You don't understand now—there's no way you could. But your crew crashing on T'Kani Prime changed everything. All I want is a chance to help you fix your mistake, Buzz. To go back in time—to set things right."

"But why?" Buzz asked. "Why do you want to help me?"

Zurg paused. "Let's just say—our interests are aligned."

Buzz shook his head, confusion clouding his judgment. "I don't understand."

"You don't need to." Zurg took a step closer. "All

you need to see is that together, we can go back in time to change things."

"You mean . . ." Buzz trailed off, processing what Zurg was suggesting. "You mean I can stop my crew from ever landing on that planet?"

Zurg nodded. "You can stop yourself from ever hitting that mountain."

Slowly, Buzz lowered his wrist laser. He knew he couldn't—shouldn't—trust this mysterious Zurg. But this offer was a possibility Buzz had never imagined.

"We can just continue the mission home," Buzz said, the truth dawning on him.

"And none of this will have ever happened," Zurg added. The robot held up Buzz's glowing fuel cell. "This crystal is the key to it all. With this, we can travel through time."

"But you said you've already traveled through time," Buzz pointed out. "So, don't you already have a crystal?"

Zurg chuckled. "Well . . . sort of."

Zurg led Buzz down a long hall to a room surrounded by screens. Various robots worked busily around the perimeter, operating the consoles. In the center was a plasma engine, powered by a dimly glowing fuel crystal, just like Buzz's.

"See, I wore my crystal out testing the time travel," Zurg explained. "But then I realized I could just get a brand-new crystal from you."

Buzz eyed the engine curiously. Its setup looked vaguely familiar, as though he intuitively knew how to control it. But was any of this truly possible? Could he really travel back in time and stop the crash? He wanted so badly to believe what Zurg was saying, that his mistake could be fixed before it ever happened. But none of this made sense.

"Tell me why you want to help me," Buzz insisted. "Why do you want to change the past?"

The robot held its arms wide. "I can't give you all the answers you want, Buzz. But trust me when I say, we want the same thing. Just a chance to make things right. You spent a lifetime trying to fix your mistake without the right tools. I'm giving you those tools. I'm giving you that chance."

Buzz thought about it. All this time, he had been so focused on finding a stable fuel source. But what if the answer had never been hyperspeed in the first place? What if time travel was the only true option for success, the missing piece to the puzzle for which he had been searching so long?

"It's a good plan," he said quietly.

Together, they began working at the engine console, flipping switches in unison like a well-oiled machine, preparing to swap in the fresh fuel crystal.

"You know," Buzz said, reminiscing. "There's an old friend of mine who will finally get her wish because of this." He thought fondly of Alisha. "She'll get to be a Space Ranger again." Buzz's hand paused midair over a switch, the multicolored glow of the fuel crystal reflecting off his white gauntlet. "Though . . . ," he said slowly, "she won't have her family. She won't have Izzy."

Zurg removed the old crystal from the fuel housing before noticing that Buzz had stopped his work. "Buzz," Zurg said in a deep voice. "Nobody's going to remember any of this. The only thing anybody's going to know is that you finished your mission."

Zurg tossed the used crystal aside and held out a robotic hand.

"Here, hand me your crystal," Zurg directed.

Buzz furrowed his brow. Was it fair to erase all those people down there so that his crew might have the chance to go home? Was it fair to erase Izzy?

"I don't know," Buzz said, unsure. "Maybe . . . maybe we should think about this."

"Think about what?" Zurg spat. "You just said your friend would get her wish."

"Yeah, but . . . she had a whole life down there," Buzz replied.

"Believe me, you don't want to live like this," Zurg said. "Reliving the nightmare. Haunted by your mistake. You can finally let go of that. Starting right now."

Zurg held out a hand for the crystal again. And Buzz studied it for a long moment.

It was true: Buzz had made mistakes. A lot of them. But the life Alisha built hadn't been a mistake. Her smile in Sox's hologram and all the times Buzz had returned from his missions hadn't been because she was dreaming of what couldn't be. She had been smiling for what *was*. Her life, her family, everything she had built with her own two hands. Crashing on T'Kani Prime may not have been the plan. But maybe, just maybe, it wasn't a mistake after all.

Buzz looked up at Zurg with renewed confidence.

"You're right," said Buzz. "I can." He lowered the fuel crystal to his side and walked toward the door.

"Where are you going?" Zurg demanded.

"I've spent far too long trapped in the past. Maybe my mission is to make a better future for the people down there, now." Buzz squared his shoulders. "I won't help you."

Zurg's eyes glowed a deeper red than Buzz thought possible.

"Then you leave me no choice."

Far below on T'Kani Prime, Izzy, Darby, and Mo sat forlornly by the powerless Armadillo.

"Hey, cat," Darby called to Sox. "Do you know how to fly this thing?"

"Um, there's no fuel," Sox replied.

Mo pulled at his hair. "See, *this* is why we should have never gotten in over our heads."

"What did *you* want to do?" Darby snapped. "Wait at the outpost until the robots found us?"

"Well, that's better than being stranded out here, where no one's *ever* going to find us!" Mo shouted back.

While they bickered, Izzy simply sat. She'd never felt emptiness like this before. Not only had she let down her team, but she had let down her grandmother's best friend and gotten him captured in the process. She was supposed to be a leader, like her grandmother. Some Hawthorne she'd turned out to be.

Frustrated, Izzy ripped the Hawthorne nameplate off her suit and tossed it on the ground.

Sox padded up to her. "I've completely lost Buzz," he said sadly. "He's too far away to track."

Izzy sighed. Buzz was probably up on that Zurg ship right now, enduring who knew what. She stared blankly at the nameplate on the ground, the wind picking it up and carrying it away, toward the Armadillo. At that moment, she noticed something on the ship. What she saw made her gasp.

"Everybody! Inside!" she ordered.

"What?" Darby asked, stopping in the middle of a verbal tirade against Mo.

"What's after us now?" Mo looked around nervously as they all clambered up and into the ship.

"We don't have any more weapons!" Darby pointed out.

"That's okay," Izzy said, her voice fueled with renewed confidence. "We're getting out of here."

"Where are we going?" Sox asked.

Izzy leaned out the Armadillo window, looking at the transport disc one of the robots had slapped on it.

"We're going to space."

She took a deep breath and slammed a fist against the button. The ship disappeared.

Chapter 14

"No, you can't do this!" Buzz resisted as two robots restrained him. "You're going to erase it all!"

Zurg's eyes flashed as the robot strode over and picked up the glowing fuel crystal. "Exactly."

"You're going to take away people's families!" Buzz exclaimed. "Their friends. *My* friends. They have lives on that planet. Everyone does!"

"I hardly recognize you, Buzz," said Zurg. "All these new ideas . . . you know what? We'll go ahead and erase those, too."

Zurg's hand reached toward the launch button.

"No!" screamed Buzz.

At that moment, he broke free from the robots and blasted them with his laser. One robot toppled into Zurg, causing the foe to drop the fuel crystal and crash into the control panel.

Buzz sprang forward, grabbed hold of the fuel crystal, and sprinted out of the room.

He had to make his way to the bridge. Operation Surprise Party was back on.

He was going to blow up the ship.

In the transport room, an unlikely quartet appeared in a blinding flash of light. Izzy, Mo, Darby, and Sox had all teleported in the Armadillo up to Zurg's ship.

"Operation Surprise Party, here we go!" Izzy said eagerly as they climbed out. She looked at her team.

"Hup, hup!" they all said in unison.

"We need to protect our escape ship," Izzy directed, taking control like a real Space Ranger, feeling the strength of her grandma coursing through her. "If the robots get to it, we'll never get out alive. So nothing comes through that door."

Darby pointed to herself and Mo. "Don't worry. We'll seal it off."

"You go find Buzz," Mo said, their confidence inspiring him, too.

"I'll track the chip in his dog tags," Sox confirmed, his ears tracking the signal. "Come on!"

"And I've got us a shortcut back." Izzy grabbed a transport disc from the wall and slapped it on her back.

With that, she and Sox slipped out of the transport

room and stealthily hurried down the long corridor in the direction of Buzz's signal.

"Meow, meow, meow, meow," Sox repeated softly as he continued homing in on his target. "Oh! The signal is tighter now. He has to be straight this way!"

He led Izzy to a glass-windowed observatory, giving her a first real glimpse of the vastness of space outside the ship. Izzy stopped and gulped.

"*Bguhhh.* That's a lot of space." She felt a knot forming in her stomach and looked down at the floor so she wouldn't throw up. "Keep it together . . . keep it together," she whispered to herself.

Suddenly, alarms sounded. Something had triggered the ship's security system! Izzy heard robots thundering toward the transport room just as the door behind them slid shut with a resounding *thunk.* They were trapped!

"No, no, no!" Izzy pounded on the door.

Sox looked around, confused. "I don't understand. The signal says Buzz is fifty meters away."

Izzy begrudgingly turned her gaze back toward the windows, breathing rhythmically to keep herself calm. It was like being trapped in a fishbowl surrounded by her greatest fear. Beyond the glass barrier of the observatory windows was nothing but the immense black void of space—except for a portion of the ship that jutted out directly across from them. Izzy pressed her hands against the glass and gasped.

"He's over there!" She pointed to the bridge, where Buzz was standing at the control panel.

And he wasn't alone.

Over on the bridge, Buzz tried to make sense of the futuristic command console. Unlike the plasma engine from before, none of it looked familiar. "I don't know any of this technology," he said, frustrated. For the first time in his life, he wished he had an auto-pilot to tell him what to do.

"Computer, is there an autopilot?" he asked hopefully.

"Affirmative," the computer replied. "You may call me IVAN."

"IVAN—" Buzz whispered. What were the odds that Zurg's ship ran on exactly the same autopilot that Star Command used?

What was Zurg not telling him?

"IVAN," Buzz instructed, taking a chance. "Initiate self-destruct sequence in two minutes."

"Self-destruct countdown initiated," IVAN replied.

Buzz turned—and was immediately caught in a chokehold by Zurg.

"Enough!" Zurg bellowed, pulling Buzz painfully close. "Just tell me where the crystal is."

Zurg flung Buzz across the room, slamming the Space Ranger hard into a console. Buzz's head throbbed upon impact. He rolled down to the floor, and suddenly realized he wasn't rolling at all—he was hovering.

Dazed, he looked over at the control panel. He'd accidentally hit the antigravity button. Now everything was starting to float up and around the bridge, including the fuel crystal, which Zurg caught sight of. The menacing robot chuckled.

"No!" yelled Buzz. He fired his wrist laser, but his focus was still woozy. He missed, instead hitting an energy transformer behind Zurg, which exploded like a shock wave. Both Zurg and Buzz were blasted to opposite sides of the bridge. Zurg's red eyes flickered, and Buzz slammed into a window. He felt his vision dimming as he floated listlessly beside a glass panel that offered a glimpse into the vast darkness of space.

"Buzz?"

The voice seemed to be coming from outside. No—his communicator.

"Are you okay?" the voice asked.

Buzz blinked and looked out the window in a stupor. He couldn't make sense of what he was seeing.

Across the way was a glass observatory jutting out from the ship, and pressed against the glass window, watching him, was Alisha.

"No, Alisha." His own voice sounded distant. "I—I need help."

"Buzz, I'm not my grandma," the woman said.

Buzz shook the cobwebs from his brain. He squinted. The woman watching him wasn't Alisha at all, but Izzy. Somehow, she had made it to the ship. Somehow, she had made it there to help him—all on her own.

"Izzy," Buzz said, "I don't need your grandma. I need *you*."

Chapter 15

In the observatory, Izzy desperately searched for escape options. "How do we get over there?"

Sox scanned the room. "Through the air lock."

Izzy looked to where Sox indicated and felt her chest seize up in panic. The cat wanted her to walk through a door leading into space! "Through *there?*" she exclaimed. "There's *nothing* out there!"

"Exactly," explained Sox. "Nothing in your way. You just go straight across."

Izzy stared across to the other section of the ship. Sox was right—an identical air lock was on that side. Theoretically, if she jumped out from this one, she would float straight across to the other. Unless she missed, and just kept drifting out into space—forever.

Izzy looked back at Buzz. He was still floating limply near the glass window on the bridge. It looked like his eyes were closed.

He needs me, Izzy thought, pushing down the fear

rising in her. *I have to do this—he's running out of time!*

Taking deep, rhythmic breaths, Izzy and Sox climbed into the air lock, and she sealed the door to the observatory behind them. Then Izzy lowered her helmet's face shield and Sox climbed up onto her back. With a shaking hand, she pressed the release button for the outer air lock door.

WHOOOOSH.

Her worst fear lay stretched before her: an infinite abyss of simply—nothing. Nothing to grab hold of. Nothing to save her if she drifted off-course. Endless emptiness.

"Just don't look down," Sox instructed.

Izzy looked up, and the same view greeted her above. It was a void so black, she felt it could suck her in if she stared too long.

"Or up," Sox said quickly. "It's all space. It's everywhere. All around you. I'm sorry. I'm probably not helping. Just go straight. Once you push off, that's the direction you'll go."

Izzy gulped. "But what if I miss?"

"Don't miss," Sox said.

With a final deep breath, Izzy aimed for the bridge air lock, ready to push off.

Every fiber of her being told her not to do this. But this wasn't about her. It was about her friend. Only she could save him.

Don't let go, her pounding heart seemed to say.

Izzy let go.

Back on the bridge, Buzz saw the fuel cell floating an arm's length away. He pushed past the pain and forced himself to regain focus. Using the window as leverage, he propelled himself forward and swam toward the fuel cell.

Buzz just barely managed to grab hold of the fuel cell as he drifted past the main console. From the corner of his eye, he could see the countdown: only twenty-five seconds left. Somehow, he had to get away from Zurg, reach Izzy, and get them off this ship before it was too late.

Twisting in the air, he pushed himself toward the bridge door. He was halfway there when he felt an unexpected lurch in his stomach and slammed to the ground.

"Ugh!" Buzz landed heavily on his arm. He managed to hold on to the fuel cell, but his wrist blaster broke off and skidded across the floor. He lifted his head and saw Zurg standing triumphantly by the main console, the artificial gravity reinstated.

Zurg pushed another few buttons and the computer chimed, "Manual override activated."

Zurg chuckled as Buzz realized that the self-destruct sequence had paused with only ten seconds remaining.

Suddenly, the air lock door at their side crashed open. Zurg whipped around to face it. But no one was there—the air lock was empty.

In that moment of confusion, Buzz reached out to grab his wrist blaster. But he wasn't quick enough. Zurg saw what was happening and extended a robotic hand to snare Buzz in a squeeze so tight, he could barely breathe.

Then something inexplicable happened. A figure materialized out of thin air in the middle of the bridge. Buzz watched in disbelief as Izzy became visible, leaving stealth mode, with Sox on her shoulder, and they were right next to his fallen wrist blaster. She had made it across—and they had one shot.

"Now!" Buzz gasped.

Knowing exactly what to do, Izzy snatched up the wrist blaster and threw it just as Buzz stretched out his hand. It was the perfect throw and catch. Buzz gripped the blaster and fired down at the cord attaching Zurg's hand to the bot's arm. In a spray of sparks, the cord severed, and the recoil sent Zurg reeling back over the main console. Buzz somersaulted down to the floor, still cradling the precious fuel crystal.

Without so much as a breath, he sprinted forward and grabbed Izzy.

"Come on!" he shouted. "Let's get out of here!"

Izzy pointed to the console. "We have to blow up the ship!"

"There's no time!" Buzz shook his head. "We'll never make it."

"Oh yes, we will," Izzy said with the confidence of a true Space Ranger, producing the transport disc she'd found.

Buzz felt a surge of pride. With a nod, he aimed his wrist blaster at the self-destruct button on the main console and fired.

"Self-destruct sequence reactivated," IVAN announced. "Resuming countdown. Ten . . . nine . . ."

Behind the console, Zurg rose like a monolith, livid at what was happening. "IVAN?" the robot bellowed, intending to shut down the self-destruct again. But IVAN didn't respond.

Zurg's eyes burned like lava as they peered down and the robot realized the console panel was ruined, and the self-destruct sequence was locked in.

"IVAN!" Zurg roared.

But Buzz, Izzy, and Sox weren't there to witness the full wrath of Zurg, because they had already used the transport disc to disappear.

Chapter 16

"What happened in here?" Izzy exclaimed as she, Buzz, and Sox reappeared on top of the Armadillo in the transport room and slid down the side. Darby and Mo stood before a smoking pile of robot wreckage that blocked the entry door to the transport room.

"I sealed the door," Darby said bluntly. "Like you asked."

"See, we triggered the alarm," Mo explained hurriedly. "And then all the robots came. But Darby then found three things, and—"

"Boom." Darby nodded.

"Well, there's about to be an even bigger boom," Buzz urged. "Everyone, get in!"

Izzy, Darby, Mo, and Sox clambered aboard the ship as Buzz hastily went to insert the fuel crystal. He had just opened the fuel door, when—

KA-BOOM!

They were too late! The self-destruct sequence had started. An explosion rocked Zurg's ship, and the entire vessel listed to one side. Buzz lost his grip on the Armadillo and began sliding down toward an open cargo bay door. He just barely managed to grab hold of the fuel crystal and activate his Space Ranger helmet before he passed through the pressurization force field and out into open space. Everything from the transport room—the deactivated robots, the Armadillo, Buzz's XL-15 ship—all tumbled out into the void and began to drift.

The force of the blast sent everything hurtling down toward T'Kani Prime, including Buzz. Free-falling through space, he collided with the XL-15, bouncing off the hull. Buzz reached out wildly and snagged the edge of the ship's wing just before he went flying off into deep space. Straining with every fiber in his body, Buzz heaved himself up and onto the ship, clinging to it for dear life. He could see the fuel port.

Inch by inch, he pulled himself toward the small door, even while all about him fiery debris from the crash sailed by, threatening to knock him loose at any moment. His fingers closed around the fuel door handle, and he pried it open, shoving the fuel crystal into place. It activated with a hum of energy, powering up the ship. Breathing hard, Buzz pulled himself to the cockpit and climbed inside. The canopy whooshed closed, and the ship pressurized. Sweat drenched the inside of Buzz's Space Ranger suit. He had done it.

Now he had to save his friends. Without a fuel source, they were helpless against the gravitational pull of the planet. They would get sucked into the upper atmosphere and crash down to the surface if he didn't get to them and transfer over the fuel crystal in time.

Buzz fired up the ship's engines and locked on course for the plummeting Armadillo.

"Come on," he said through gritted teeth, pushing full throttle toward his friends.

Suddenly, the back of the ship pitched downward, like something heavy had sat on it. At first, Buzz thought he must have collided with a piece of falling wreckage. But when he turned to look, a pit formed deep in his stomach.

"Going somewhere?" a deep mechanical voice asked him.

It was Zurg! Somehow, the robot had managed to survive the self-destruct and was latched onto Buzz's ship!

Zurg laughed, ripping off the back wing and hurling it into space. Inside, Buzz struggled to keep control, but it was no use. The ship started spiraling. Zurg reached the fuel port and wrenched the fuel cell from it, which shut down the thrusters and the weapons. Buzz was out of power and out of defenses. Only the ship's emergency lights retained residual energy—along with one glowing red button Buzz recognized all too well.

An eject button.

"Don't be scared, Buzz," Zurg's voice echoed as the foe crept along the hull to face Buzz, its burning red eyes practically searing a hole through the windshield. "I'm going to erase all this, remember? You could have used this crystal to matter again. Instead, it will be like you were never here. So . . . prepare to die."

Buzz locked eyes with Zurg—and hit the glowing red eject button. The back of his seat strapped around him, and the ship's canopy burst open, launching Buzz from the cockpit. The seat back opened to reveal a jet pack with wings! Buzz flipped up and over Zurg, flying out in front of the careening ship. Zurg turned just in time to see Buzz take aim with his wrist blaster at the glowing crystal clutched in Zurg's hands.

"Not today, Zurg!" Buzz exclaimed.

With that, Buzz fired his laser and blasted the crystal.

"No!" Zurg screamed.

The crystal exploded in a blaze of color that was brighter than Buzz had ever witnessed, engulfing

Zurg along with it. The culmination of a hundred years of work—gone in one brilliant explosion.

But all that was in the past now. Buzz had a new mission.

He aimed himself toward the Armadillo and engaged his jet pack, shooting forward on an intercept course to save his friends.

"We've entered the planet's gravitational pull," Sox alerted everyone as the Armadillo careened toward certain doom.

"Are we gonna crash?" Mo asked.

"I'm afraid so," Sox replied.

Izzy, Darby, and Mo exchanged frightened whimpers. This wasn't looking good.

Then like a miracle, Buzz Lightyear sailed in front of the ship!

"Buzz!" Izzy cried, pressing against the windshield. She couldn't believe it—Buzz was alive!

Buzz positioned himself in front of the Armadillo and pushed his jet pack to full power. Without a fuel crystal, his only hope for getting the ship under control was to slow its descent. But even he knew that the odds of success were slim. One little jet pack hardly had the firepower to match up to the gravitational pull of T'Kani Prime. He pushed with all his might, the metal nose of the Armadillo crushing under the pressure. But the ship didn't slow.

Buzz looked at his friends through the windshield. Their expectant faces plainly showed all their hopes were pinned on him. He wanted so badly not to let them down.

"I—" His voice broke. "I can't do it."

Izzy studied his face for a long beat, and then, inexplicably, she smiled.

"Hey! That's all right," she told him. "*We* can!"

Now it was Buzz's turn to look hopeful.

"Can you keep the ship steady?" Izzy asked him.

"Affirmative," Buzz replied. He zoomed under the Armadillo's hull and grabbed two handholds, using the power of his jet pack to guide the ship more steadily. "Sox," he said into his communicator. "Use your emergency battery to power up flight controls!"

"Got it!" Sox replied. The robotic cat lifted his tail and the end popped off, revealing the flash drive. He inserted the drive into the main console, activating the emergency battery. The ship's controls sprang to life.

"I'll need a copilot," Izzy said, looking at Mo.

"Okay . . . I've only done this in the simulator," Mo said hesitantly.

"Well, it's about to get real," Izzy told him as they

took their seats. She reminded him to pull back on the control wheel nice and easy.

Mo yanked the control wheel back much too hard, and a flap on the right wing ripped off, whizzing past Buzz's head.

Izzy shot Mo a look, and he grimaced. "Yep, sorry. Nice and easy from now on."

All around them, the ship began to glow from the heat of reentry into the planet's atmosphere. Not for the first time, Buzz was grateful for the protection of his Space Ranger suit. But their efforts still weren't enough. Buzz turned to his last remaining hope.

"IVAN?" he called out.

"Yes, captain?" said IVAN, full of static.

"We're going too fast!"

"Congratulations!" IVAN exclaimed. Confetti shot out of the dash.

"We don't need confetti! We need brakes!" Mo exclaimed.

"The air brake!" Izzy and Buzz shouted in realization.

"IVAN, is there an air brake?" Izzy asked.

"Certainly," IVAN replied. "The air brake is located on the floor."

Izzy looked around and spotted the air brake under a cover on the floor. "Darby!" she exclaimed.

Darby bent down and hit a button to open the air brake cover. But it was jammed.

"The cover! It's stuck! I need a screwdriver . . . or a hair clip . . . or some sort of a small wedge."

Mo's eyes brightened with a sudden realization. "The pen! I've got the pen!"

He popped the pen out of his suit and wielded it like a sword. He leaned over and pried open the cover, allowing Darby to pull on the air brake with force and fury.

Finally, the ship began to slow. Its descent was still incredibly fast. But with everyone working together, they had a chance.

The wind whipped past as the ground raced up to meet the ship. Buzz let go at the last possible second, watching the Armadillo sail forward mere feet above the ground before it scraped across the surface in a massive wave of dirt, rock, and burned metal.

Slowly, the Armadillo skidded to a stop, coming to a rest long before the team's pounding hearts did.

Buzz used his jet pack to loop overhead and touch down.

"Is everyone okay?" he shouted, sprinting up to the door. Shaking, Izzy, Darby, Mo, and Sox emerged from the ship. Then they all embraced Buzz in a group hug that was fiercer than any alien force in the universe.

Suddenly, the sound of sirens broke through the team's emotional moment.

"The cops! Everyone run!" Darby cried.

"Wait . . . it's just the rescue team," Buzz said.

"Oh, right. Okay," said Darby, relieved.

"You know, you seem like a decent citizen," Buzz said. "What led to your incarceration?"

"I stole a ship," Darby replied.

"Oh. I see," Buzz said, uncomfortable. "Well, you know, who among us hasn't stolen a ship in a moment of relative desperation?"

Mo walked over to them, holding his pen aloft. "I am a man of resources! My weapon is ingenuity! I can do anything!"

"Can you not shout in my ear?" Darby said.

Buzz glanced over at Izzy, who was looking up at the sky with a soft smile on her face.

"You okay?" Buzz asked.

Izzy pointed up. "I was in space."

Buzz squeezed Izzy's shoulder. "Your grandma would be proud."

Izzy looked at Buzz appreciatively. His praise meant more to her than anything in the world, because coming from him, she knew she'd earned it.

"She'd be proud of you, too," Izzy said. "She always was." Then Izzy realized Buzz was missing something very important. "Wait, where's your crystal?"

Buzz simply shook his head. "It's gone."

"But your mission . . . ," Izzy insisted. "You wanted to go home."

"You know," said Buzz, looking at his team, "for the first time in a long time, I feel like I *am* home."

Chapter 17

"Lightyear!" Commander Burnside said sternly.

Buzz stood at attention as the commander paced in front of him. The Space Ranger was prepared for a dressing-down that was twenty-two years in the making.

"You absconded with Star Command property, stole an experimental spacecraft, and defied a direct order from your commander. I ought to throw you in the stockade."

Buzz hung his head. Commander Burnside was right—his conduct had been unbecoming of a Space Ranger. Even if he *had* saved the entire T'Kani Prime colony from annihilation.

"But I have other plans for you," Burnside told Buzz.

Burnside gestured to the deactivated robots on the ground. "We want you to start a new version of the Space Ranger Corps: Universe Protection Division.

You're going to be a Space Ranger again, Buzz. You can hand-select your team from the very best of the Zap Patrol and train them to your liking."

The security patrol saluted Buzz. "Hup, hup!"

Buzz smiled as he took in the news. To be a Space Ranger again, out among the stars. It felt like coming home. But his smile quickly faded.

"Well, that's very kind of you, sir," he said. "But . . . I'm afraid I'm going to have to decline."

Everyone looked at Buzz in shock.

"I already have my team," Buzz said, turning to look at Izzy, Darby, Mo, and Sox.

The doors of the launch bay opened, revealing a team of Space Rangers outfitted in new, state-of-the-art suits. As members of the Universe Protection Division of Space Ranger Corps, this elite group protected the galaxy from any sworn enemies of the Galactic Alliance. They were headed to gamma quadrant section four to investigate an unknown signal.

Darby held up her arm blaster. "I can't believe I'm allowed to carry this. I wish I had two of them."

"You got a clean record and you're free and armed," Mo said. "How are you still complaining?"

"I got off for good behavior, not good attitude," Darby replied.

"You know, I never wear pants," Sox said, looking at his new space vest, "but suddenly it feels weird not to be wearing pants. Does it look weird without pants?"

"Nah, you look good," Mo reassured him.

As the group approached a statue of Commander Alisha Hawthorne, Izzy stopped and puffed out her chest like she once did as a child in her homemade Space Ranger costume.

"Look, Grandma. I'm a Space Ranger, too. Just like you."

"She really is," Buzz said quietly to Alisha. He gave her a salute and caught up to his team.

They prepared for launch with Buzz in the pilot's seat. Behind him, Darby and Mo were strapped in, ready for takeoff. Sox was positioned in a perfect-fitting compartment on top of the console, able to plug in directly to the computer. And Izzy was the copilot at Buzz's side.

"Do we have everything?" Buzz asked. "Munitions?"

"Check," Darby said.

"Sustenance?"

"I brought sandwiches," Mo replied.

Buzz turned to Izzy, concerned. "I don't know. Am I forgetting anything?"

Izzy smiled and shook her head confidently. "I think we're ready."

Buzz nodded and inserted IVAN into the control console.

"Hello," said IVAN. "I am your Internal Voice-Activated Navigator."

Buzz smiled. "Good to have you back, IVAN."

A message from the control room came over the radio. "Captain Lightyear, ready for launch."

"IVAN," Buzz said, "initiate hyperlaunch."

"Certainly," IVAN replied. "Hyperlaunch initiating."

The ship's engines flared to life as the launch sequence initiated.

"All right, Space Rangers," Buzz declared. "Here we go."

Izzy held out a finger to Buzz with a knowing smile. "To infinity . . ."

Buzz tapped a finger to hers. ". . . and beyond."